A C

copyright 2009 by Shameek A. Speight
web address:
www.createspace.com/3418104
author's email:
shameekspeight199@gmail.com
ISBN 978-1449966126
First Edition

Dedications

I dedicate this book to my mother for believing in me, like you said mom, touch the world, but don't let it touch you. I'll touch the world one book at a time. I also dedicate this book to all the abusive women in this world, stay strong and always keep going, there's always someone depending on you.

Acknowledgments:

It has only been the power of God, my Lord and savior Jesus Christ that I have been able to persevere through many of my trials that I have been in my life. I thank him. To my family, my beloved sisters thank you for believing in me. To my auntie, I love you. To my daughter, Niomi, I do all this for you baby. To all the men and women who are locked up, hold your head and keep your faith. There will be a brighter day. To my niggas in the hood, I told you I could sell books. To Antonio Inch Thomas, thank you for teaching me all about the book game. To all my fans, thank you for all your support.

A CHILD OF A CRACKHEAD

He watched as she screamed and yelled with every strike that the man made to her face. From her mouth, she spit blood that was rolling down her face. He continued to watch the 6'2" dark skin man repeatedly hit and kick the woman in the stomach, again and again. "Bitch, I'll kill you!"

"Nooooo stop! Please stop!" as she yelled his closed fist went upside her head. She tried to get up to only be knocked right back down with a punch to her jaw. Tears and blood were mixed and were constantly running down her face. Michael knew he had to do something to stop the man from beating the beautiful brown skin woman. With tears running down his own face he yelled, "Daddy stop, daddy stop!" as he ran his 6 year old frame up in between his father and his mother. "Daddy, stop hitting mommy!" All he felt was his father's big black hands grasp him around his neck and squeeze until he couldn't breathe and threw him across the room. Michael sat on the floor crying. Partly because of the pain he felt, but mostly because of the beating his mother was getting. He again watched his

4

father repeatedly kick and hit his mother over and over. Michael eased his little body off the floor. And knew he had to help his mother, even if he got hurt again. He ran to his father's leg and wrapped himself around it and bit into his father's thigh with all his might. "Aahhh, you little fucker!" he yelled as he tried to shake Michael off his leg. But, Michael held on with his arms squeezing tighter and his teeth locked down in his father's leg. Until he was struck on his back so hard, he couldn't breathe. Michael gasped for air. "Don't hit my son!" Michael's mother yelled. And with quick reaction she jabbed the big man in the eye, "Aahhh! You bitch, Rachel, I'm going to kill you!" he yelled while holding his eye. She got up off the floor and slid up underneath the bed. The big hand tried to grab her, but his hand wouldn't fit under the bed. He lifted the bed over his head to see his woman rounded up into a ball, shaking under the bed frame. He smiled with a devilish grin and bent down to grab her. The man felt pain from his hand. He looked at the blood that was running down his hand. He kept trying to grab for Rachel, but with every reach he received the same pain came again and again. Blood was everywhere. In a swift move, Rachel got up and started swinging wild. Blood was flying everywhere with each hit she struck him with. He noticed then that it wasn't her blood. It was his. He was feeling the pain in every spot on his arms and hands where she struck him. While he used his arms to defend her strike, he tried to focus his attention on what she had in her hands. It was too late. The razor came down and sliced his face. Splitting his cheek to the white meat, turning pink and blood just poured from the thick long cut. He bent down and yelled in anger and pain. Rachel took the only opportunity she had and grabbed Michael and ran out the door. They lived on the fifth floor of an apartment building. She held her son with both arms wrapped around him. She ran down the stars as fast as she possibly could in complete terror and badly hurt and hoping she wouldn't drop Michael. She made it to the apartment buildings lobby. The exit was right in front of her. Thinking and smiling with relief that she had made it. Her neck snapped back with a powerful force and was taken down to the floor with Michael still wrapped around her. She screamed as loud as she could, but no one would come out of their apartment doors to help them. Michael looked back to see that the long black hand reached and grabbed his mother's hair and drug them all the way back up the stairs into their apartment where he and his mother received the beating of their lives. What seemed like an endless night of destruction to the apartment and beatings to Rachel and Michael, not one person in the apartment building that heard the screams and cries for help would come to help and save them.

Chapter 2

Rachel watched as her husband left the apartment. She got up and began to clean up the mess in the apartment and clean her wounds. She walked over to her son and gently wiped his face with a clean hot rag. "Oww mommy it hurts!" Michael cried when she touched the knot on his head with the rag. "Jr., I have to clean you up. I know it hurts, but you have to be my big man."

"Yes, mommy," Michael said. "Mommy, I hate him! Why do I have to have the same name as him? I don't want to be like him."

"Baby, you'll never be like him. Always remember, a woman is like a flower. Flowers are to be treated only with a gentle touch. Knowing that, you should always treat women with a gentle touch, love her, and cherish her."

"Yes mommy."

"You always remember that Jr."

"I hate him, mommy."

"He's not that bad Jr. It's the drugs. When he smokes that stuff, it messes with his head. He gets mad and does things like this. He gets mad at me when I don't want to smoke it with him and beats me."

Michael really didn't understand what he

8

was just told. But, all he knew was his father acted funny and crazy after smoking the funny smelling stuff in what looked like a glass pipe.

Michael Ice Sr., or better known on the streets as "Black Ice", was feared by everyone and anybody everywhere he went. Most people that heard the name, Black Ice, thought he got the name because of his black skin that shined like a beautiful black jewel. But, those that knew the real reason feared him a great deal. Michael Ice, Sr. had a cold heart. When he was younger the old timer's would say he was as cold as ice, just like his last name. So the name stuck with him. Black Ice had two drug spots in east New York Brooklyn. He was the man and could get whatever he wanted—women, clothes, and jewelry. What he didn't have he would take. His life was smooth, or the shit, as he would put it. Shit started going downhill for Black Ice once he started fucking around with a broad named, Roxy. Roxy was sexy as fuck. She had a fat ass, light skin complexion, and a body most women would die for. She wanted nothing to do with a drug dealer. She was in school studying to be a nurse. Black Ice had the love of his life, his wife Rachel, and the mother of his child. Even with that, he still wanted to have a taste of Roxy. He came up with a plan. He knew that Roxy loved to smoke weed. And one day Black Ice asked her if she wanted to go smoke with him. Roxy looked at Black Ice funny. She thought he was a sexy, black mother fucker, but she couldn't get messed up with a drug dealer. Then she thought to herself, what would it hurt to get high with him? And she thought even if she did, she would have control the whole time. When she agreed, Black Ice took her to one of his many apartments he owned in Brooklyn. He rolled up a blunt and gave it to Roxy who was sitting on the couch with her thick, sexy legs crossed. Roxy lit the blunt and moaned as she inhaled. "This is some good ass shit." She hit the blunt three more times and passed it back to Black Ice. He hesitated on taking the blunt. Roxy lifted her left eyebrow and looked at him, "What you're not going to smoke with me?" Black Ice knew that he had to hit the blunt or she'd think something was wrong. Black Ice laced the weed with crack and didn't want to hit it, but knew he had too. As he hit the blunt hard and passed it right back to Roxy he thought to himself that he would be able to handle it. "Damn,

I'm high as a kite. I have never gotten this high before," Roxy said as she continued to smoke and pass the blunt back and forth between them. Roxy was getting horny and she couldn't quite understand why her pussy was getting wet. She started rubbing on her breast with her hand through her shirt. Black Ice noticed her playing with herself and knew that this was his opportunity to get that taste of Roxy he so fantasized about. He moved in closer to Roxy on the couch and began kissing on her neck very softly. Roxy tilted her head and he then sucked her neck. Roxy let out a little moan. Black Ice moved up to her lips and began kissing her. Their tongues danced in each other's mouths. He pulled up her shirt and looked at her beautiful, full breasts. He circled her nipples with his tongue. "Yes, yes!" Roxy moaned as Black Ice pulled down her jeans and panties. He kissed and licked her from her lips to her neck and down her body between her thighs. Spreading her legs gently apart and with every turn of his head there were her thick thighs and her wet ass pussy right in front of him. He slowly kissed her inner thighs with soft, gentle wet kisses. "Yes, ohhh, yes baby," she bit her bottom lip as his tongue made its way to her

11

clit. Roxy eyes rolled back as he pushed his tongue inside her pussy. He savored her sweet taste. Roxy's body began to tremble with each movement of his tongue that teased and pleased her inside. She began rocking her hips and rubbing her breast with one hand and fondling her clit with the other. Black Ice pulls himself up to glance at Roxy to see how engaged she was in what was happening. He wanted to see what she would do once he used his fingers inside her like it was his own dick penetrating inside her. She gave out a loud moan, thrusting her hips, and licking her lips. Her vaginal muscles contracted with every move his finger made inside her. He went back down and licked her pussy and put his tongue back inside her only for a moment. He couldn't take her sweet moans any more. His dick was getting as hard as a rock. He stood up over Roxy who still kept fondling herself and moaning after his tongue came out of her. He began to undress from his shirt and jeans. Roxy was watching him undress to unveil his black, chocolate body. At 6'2" tall and 200 pounds, Black Ice was all muscle from head to toe from all the years of working out going back and forth to jail. She gasped and arched her back as he slid into her. Black Ice wasted no time to tear into that pussy that he has desired so. He had been, wanting Roxy for a long time. He put her legs on his shoulders and penetrated inside her, thrusting in and out. She moaned with each hard and deep thrust making her ass smack up against him. "Tell me this is my pussy now!" Black Ice demanded as he pulled out his nine inch dick out of her, tapping it against her pussy. "It's yours baby, yes, oh yes!" Roxy moaned. Black Ice flipped her over on the couch putting her face down in the pillow and arched her back putting her ass up in the air. He slid into her wet pussy and began to pound and pound away as his dick went deeper and deeper with every pump. "Yes baby, yes! Fuck me, fuck me!" Roxy moaned as Black Ice tore her inside up. He was intoxicated by her wetness. He smacked her ass and watched it jiggle from the back to the front. Tears of pleasure rolled down Roxy's face as she came.

"Oh, oh, ahh baby" she moaned as she climaxed. She grabbed the couch pillow and bit down on it. This only turned on Black Ice even more. He gritted his teeth as his dick throbbed and proceeded to bang her back out. His nut was building up. He pulled his dick out and turned Roxy to him and came all over her face. "Shit, that was good!" Roxy said while licking and wiping the cum from her face. "Yea, your pussy is the shit" Black Ice replied.

"You got some more weed like we just had?" Roxy asked. "Yes Mami," Black Ice rolled up another blunt full of crack and weed. He and Roxy smoked, and they fucked each other over and over again. Going back and forth from smoking and fucking, they just started smoking the crack straight up in a pipe and continued all night long.

Chapter 3

After beating Rachel's ass for not
wanting to smoke crack with him, Black Ice
jumped into his 1990 Lexus ES that just
came out that year. His drug business was
doing well for him. He grabbed a rag out of
his back seat and put it on his face to stop
the bleeding from the deep cut Rachel gave
him. "That bitch!" Black Ice said out loud.
He took out a bag full of crack cocaine and
pulled a clear pipe out of his pocket and
emptied two into the pipe. He pulled out his
lighter and flicked it and held the fire to the
end of the pipe and inhaled the crack smoke.
He held it in until he couldn't anymore and
let it out. His head spun from the high and
his eyes popped wide open. He started the
car and headed for the hospital to get his
wounds stitched up.

From the hospital, he drove to Roxy's
apartment in Flatbush. He got the place for
her after they started fucking. He pulled up
to the building and went to the door, took
out his keys, and opened the door to the
apartment. The stink smell hit him in the
face. "Damn bitch, you don't clean this
place no more?" Black Ice yelled as he
entered. Roxy didn't answer him. Black

Ice looked around the living room to see clothes and garbage all over the floor and roaches scattering around the floor. "Damn, this bitch has fallen off," he thought. He walked to the back of the apartment looking for Roxy. He opened the bedroom door and couldn't believe what his eyes saw. Roxy was naked on her knees with her ass up in the air. A light skin, thin man with a bald head was fucking her from the back. That wasn't the worst part of it Roxy was sucking a brown skin, man's dick at the same time. The three of them were all too busy fucking that they didn't even notice Black Ice opened the bedroom door. "Bitch, suck that dick! Yeah like that," the brown skin ordered while his friend was fucking Roxy's pussy from the back. "Mmmm, mmmm," Roxy moans were getting louder even though her mouth that was full of dick. She couldn't get all what she was saying out. She stopped sucking the brown skin, man's dick and the two men switched places. "Ya'll going to hit me off with some more of that crack, right?" "Yes!" the brown man said as he entered inside her from the back. Satisfied that she was going to get some more crack, she began to suck off his bald headed, light skin friend.

Black Ice had seen enough. He went back into the living room and grabbed a pillow off the couch and went into the kitchen and took a sharp butchers knife out of the drawer. He rushed right back into the bedroom. Again, not one of them heard him re-enter the bedroom. The brown skin man's back was facing Black Ice while he was humping in and out of Roxy and the light skin, bald man had his eyes closed enjoying the deep throat Roxy was giving him. Black Ice walked quietly, but quickly, up on the brown skin guy. Black Ice grabbed the man onto the floor and pulled back his head and sliced his neck from ear to ear with the butcher knife. The man never made a sound. Blood poured out his neck as he tried to gasp for air. He grabbed his neck to try to stop the blood, but there was no use. He fell over on top of Roxy. "Nigga, what the fuck is you doing?" Roxy asked with the light skin, man's dick in her hand. She felt the warm liquid running down her back when the man's weight fell on top of her. The bald man looked up to see why Roxy stopped giving him a blowjob. When he opened his eyes he was staring right up into Black Ice's dreadful eyes. He glanced over to see his dead friend on top of Roxy. Roxy was so high she thought the dude had fallen asleep after he came on her back.

"Ahhh, who the fuck are you?" the bald man questioned Black Ice. When he asked Roxy quickly bucked her body throwing the dead man off of her. She looked back and screamed when she saw Black Ice. The light skin man jumped up and ran for his jeans, where his gun was laid. Black Ice moved with the speed of light and punched the man in the nose sending him flying back into the bed next to Roxy. Black Ice pulled out a 3.80 special from his waist band and aimed at the man on the bed.

"No, No, please man! No!" the man begged for his life, not knowing that his plea was going to a deaf mans ear and a very cold heart. Roxy was screaming and Black Ice turned and pointed the gun at her.

"Shut the fuck up, bitch! Or a bullet will go through your head!" he yelled.

Roxy got quiet and tears ran down her face. Black Ice picked up a pillow off the bed and pointed the gun back at the bald man's head.

"Listen man, please. What you want? I have money and crack in my jeans pocket," The man said.

"This isn't about any money fool."
Black Ice replied then looked at Roxy on the
bed holding herself, crying covered in blood.
"It's about her? Listen man. I didn't
know this was your woman. She said she
would fuck me and my friend for some
crack. Please, don't kill me," the man
continued to beg.
"Shut the fuck up and lay on your
stomach, now!"
"Please man!"
Black Ice smacked the man in the
nose with the butt of the gun making it
bleed.
"Ah, okay I'll do it, I'll do it. Just
don't hit me again." The man turned around
on to his stomach as his feet brushed up
against his dead, friend's body he felt the
blood on his toes. Black Ice took the pillow
and forced it on the back of the man's head.
"What you doing man?" the man
cried through the pillow.
Black Ice rose the 3.80 special and
stuck the barrel into the pillow and squeezed
the trigger twice. The bullets ripped through
the pillow and tore through the man's head
and instantly the man's body went limp.
"Ahh, ahh, ahh!" Roxy screamed.
"Bitch, don't scream now! You

19

weren't screaming when you were getting fucked by these two fools. I'll give you something to scream about you fucking whore!"

Black Ice took off his belt. Roxy screamed and got her naked body that was covered in blood off the bed. She tried to run for the door, but Black Ice grabbed her by her neck and threw her down on the floor. He punched her in the eye then the jaw.

"You want to fuck niggas in the apartment I got for you. And have nigga's dicks inside you while your four fucking months pregnant with my baby inside you!" Black Ice yelled at Roxy while repeatedly hitting her all over the body with his belt.

"Stop, please stop. I won't do it again. I promise. I promise," Roxy cried. He continued to beat her. Roxy tried to put her hands up to block the belt, but he just whipped her hands. She screamed and screamed while he proceeded to whip her and kick her all over her body. Black Ice was making sure he was not touching her little fat stomach with his baby inside her.

"You stupid, bitch. I told you I was coming over to hit you off and you couldn't wait to get high. Nah, you had to go fuck and suck dick."

Roxy pleaded with Black Ice to stop, but he wouldn't. She could no longer defend herself as she was too weak and badly beat up. She just laid there on the floor as he continued to whip at her body. Roxy blacked out and still could feel him strike at her with the belt.

Black Ice left Roxy unconscious, swelling, and bleeding body on the floor and went into the living room and picked up his cell phone. He dialed Ace's number.

"What's good?" Ace answered.

"I need you and Caesar to get over here and clean up a mess for me," Black Ice demanded speaking in code.

"Where are you at?" Ace asked.

"I'm at Roxy's place and make it fast!"

"Yeah, boss. We'll be there in a few minutes."

With that said, Black Ice hung up the phone. He sat on the couch and took out his pipe from his pocket and grabbed a glass jar packed with crack and poured some into the pipe and lit it up.

Chapter 4

Black Ice smoked and got high for a half an hour until her heard a knock at the door. He walked to the door with his gun in his hand and opened it.

"What up, boss?" Ace said and walked in followed by Ceasar.

"What the fuck took you two so long?"

"I had to find Caesar. He was on the block watching the workers." Ace replied.

Black Ice raised his gun and pointed it at the two men.

"The next time I call you two and you don't come fast enough I will put a bullet in your heads. Are we clear?"

"Yes, yes boss," Ace and Caesar replied.

Ace and Caesar ran Black Ice's drug spots. Ace was a fat, short dude with dark skin and did anything Black Ice told him to do. Caesar was a tall, slender man with short dreads in his hair and he hated when Black Ice punks him, but wasn't foolish enough to open his mouth to Black Ice.

"Follow me," Black Ice said.

The two men followed him to the bedroom. Once they got there, they felt as they wanted to throw up. There was blood everywhere. The two men's dead bodies on the bed and Roxy laid naked on the floor covered in blood, bruises, and welts.

"Stop fucking looking around and stuff these two niggas into the garbage bags."

Ace pulled out some black garbage bags. Caesar and Ace grabbed one of the man's legs that were lying at the end of the bed. They pulled the dead body off the bed. The blood smeared down the bed and onto the floor. They wrapped the bags around the body and took another bag and wrapped it again. They went to the head of the bed to remove the pillow off the other dead body before wrapping it up. The pillow was stuck to the man's head with blood that started to dry to the pillow. Ace pulled it off him and Caesar grabbed his stomach at the sight he just saw. The back of the man's head was blown off with a baseball size hole in it. They grabbed the man's hands and pulled him off onto the floor onto his back.

"Holy shit, ah shit!" Caesar shouted at the sight of the man's face. His face was gone and was replaced with a big hole that you could see through. The only thing left to his face was his lips and chin.

"Shut up! Finish wrapping that mother fucker! You two are acting like you never seen a fucking dead body before!" Black Ice scorned.

Black Ice walked over to where the two men's clothes were laying after getting naked to fuck Roxy. He emptied their pockets taking all the money, crack, and the two guns, a 3.80 and a 22 handgun, and put it in his pockets.

Caesar and Ace were done wrapping the bodies and started throwing anything with blood on it in the bedroom in a garbage bag.

"What about her?" Caesar asked pointing at Roxy's naked body on the floor thinking she was dead too.

"Nigga, if you touch her it will be you next being wrapped up in a garbage bag, fool," Black Ice said looking him in his eyes meaning every word.

"Yes, I understand," Caesar replied as he and Ace took the first body to the car. They came back for the last one.

"Dump that shit in Coney Island Ocean," Black Ice ordered as Ace and Caesar left.

They jumped in their car, unnoticed by the night sky. Black Ice walked back into the bedroom towards Roxy. He took out some jars of crack and some money and put it on the bed and looked at Roxy laying there on the floor not moving at all.

"I'll be back, bitch! I know you can hear me," he said as he walked away leaving the apartment and headed for home to Rachel.

Chapter 5

Roxy lay on the floor and didn't dare move to avoid the pain even more. She was coherent the whole time Ace and Caesar were cleaning up the bedroom and wrapping the dead bodies. She watched with one eye open as the other was swollen shut and as big as golf ball. She saw Black Ice come back in the bedroom to leave her some crack and some money on the bed before he left the apartment. Tears were rolling down her swollen face as she started to wonder how she ended up in the mess she was in. Six months ago, she was going to college and studying to be a nurse while living with her mother. All she did was smoke a blunt with Black Ice that fucked up her life. As a result, she started steeling from her mother to get high. She went from smoking weed to straight crack. Black Ice promised that he would take care of her once he found out that she was pregnant with his baby after her mother kicked her out of her house. Black Ice let her move into one of the apartments he had. After that happened, that is when the beatings started to begin. He'd beat Roxy if she took too long in the bathroom or if she took too long answering him. He punched her in the jaw and giving her black eyes on her light brown skin and a swollen face. Unable to get up, Roxy just laid there and just cried and felt so empty inside. She knew she couldn't continue living the way she was. She wondered how she could quit smoking crack when it kept calling her and her body would start shaking from the actual cravings for it. And even if she found the strength to ignore the cravings, Black Ice wouldn't let her stop. She started thinking of how she could get away from him. But, she knew that he would find her and kill her if she ran away. With that thought, she just bawled and tears were streaming down her swollen face.

Chapter 6

"Push that nigga over into the water," Caesar said as Ace was rolling the body on the dock. They pushed the body over and into the water. Then went and grabbed the other body and pushed it off the dock and into the water. They watched to make sure that the bodies started to sink deep down into the ocean. It was like the ocean waves just opened up and took their bodies below.

"Come on, let's get out of here before someone sees us," Caesar said. They jumped back into the 1990 Acura Legend in a hurry to get out of there.

"Yo, that nigga is losing his damn mind!" Caesar hollered.

"Naw, Black Ice, he cool. He just gets a little crazy now and then," Ace replied.

"Nigga, are you crazy? That fool just killed those two niggas over that crack head bitch, Roxy! He was crazy before, but now that he started smoking that crack he done lost his fucking mind!" Caesar said as they pulled up to a red light.

"Yeah, you right, but what are we supposed to do?" Ace asked.

"I think Black Ice is falling out. Look

at all the weight he dropped. He went from being 230 pounds to 150 or 160 when he started smoking that shit hard up. Another thing, I'm not feeling him always pointing guns in my face. I'm tired of working for that fool. I say we take over the block. We're the ones who got the little niggas out there slanging the rock. And he takes most of the money and all he does is smoke that shit," Caesar said with anger in his voice.

"Yo, are you crazy? If Black Ice even thought we were trying to cross him, it would be us dead in Coney Island Ocean," Ace said.

"Yo, fuck that and fuck that nigga! I say we kill his ass before he kills us and we take everything. Are you in or what?"

"Yeah, I'm in." Ace said. He did want more money and Black Ice was falling off maybe they could pull it off by getting rid of him he thought. "Drop me off at my house. I'm not going back to the block tonight. I'm going to spend some time with Lisa and my kids." Ace said.

"Man, your pussy whipped. You always want to be under your girl and kids, nigga. You should be watching the block and money with me."

"Nigga please, your ass was sweating

Roxy before Black Ice got to her. I bet you'd be spending all your time with fucking her if you could," Ace said. Caesar snarled up his face with anger because he knew what Ace said was true. He wanted Roxy for a long time too. She was one of the hottest women in Brownsville. He always tried to holler at her, but she didn't want anything to do with a drug dealer. Caesar knew if he kept trying it would have been a matter of time before she gave into him. That was until Black Ice got his hands on her first and turned her into a crack head. Even as a crack head, Caesar still wanted Roxy. She was still beautiful. At that thought, a flashback ran through his mind and he remembered what he saw back at Roxy's apartment an hour earlier. Roxy was naked and her swollen body on the floor nearly beat to death. He remembered that he thought at seeing her swollen body she was dead too. Her beautiful, light brown skin body was covered in blood and bruises. How could that nigga be so evil? Caesar had thought. "Yo, when are we going to knock that nigga out? I'm going to take Roxy and clean her up and make her mines," Caesar stated.

"Nigga, now I know you're crazy!"

Ace replied as he hopped out of the car. He shut the door and walked up to his building on Shutter Avenue. Caesar pulled off heading back to the block and making up the plans to kill Black Ice off and take everything he had.

Ace went inside his apartment to see his wifey, Lisa on the couch watching TV.

"Hey baby," Lisa said when she looked up to see Ace as he leaned down and kissed her forehead. He sat down on the couch next to her.

"Where are the kids?" Ace asked.

"In their bedrooms asleep," Lisa answered.

Lisa was short and sexy. She had brown skin with long wavy hair. She only got with Ace because he had money. She didn't like the fact that he was short and fat. However, he got her out of the Brownsville Projects. He took good care of her and their two kids they had together Aaron was 5 years old and Mark was 3 years old.

Ace was in love with Lisa and told her everything. So, he started telling Lisa the discussion that Caesar and Ace were having. "Yo, this nigga, Caesar is talking some crazy shit! He's talking about killing Black Ice and taking over the drug spot's and keep all the money for ourselves. He says it's us that watch the little niggas that are slinging the rock. So, we should get all the money. Black Ice has been smoking crack and slipping. He thinks this would be the perfect time to get him. What you think, Lisa?"

Lisa, being the gold digger she is, only heard the part about the money and seeing the dollar signs. "I think it's a great idea. Shit, you and Caesar are putting all the work on these streets. You should be getting all the money. Shit, I want a house instead of an apartment. And I'm tired of you being the man under that nigga. Aren't you your own man?" Lisa asked Ace. She knew what she was doing. She was fucking with Ace's mind and making him feel less of a man. She knew that if she said the right things that would make him mad and push him over the edge to do whatever she wanted him to do.

"Yes, I'm my own man. Why you even coming at me like that?" Ace questioned.

"Nigga, I need more money for me and the kids. Shit, maybe I should have fucked with Black Ice," Lisa said.

"Yo, stop fucking playing. I'm the

man around this mother fucker. Black Ice is dead," Ace stated. Lisa knew what would motivate Ace. She got on her knees and pulled Ace's jeans down and grabbed his dick and put it in her mouth.

"Mmmm, I love it when you talk like that baby," Lisa said as she licked his dick up and down, around the head of his dick, and then surrounding his dick with deep throat. Ace moaned and watched his dick disappear inside Lisa's mouth. She slobbered and sucked his dick moving her head back and forth making Ace's eyes roll back in the back of his head. "You like that baby?" Lisa asked in between his thighs and moved her mouth back over his dick like it was going inside her pussy.

"Yes, yes, suck that shit," he moaned. Ace felt the nut building up and couldn't hold it any longer. He pulled his dick out of her mouth and jacked off all over her face. Lisa licked her lips and put his dick back into her mouth sending chills through Ace's body.

Chapter 7

Black Ice opened the door to his
family's apartment on Picking Avenue. He
closed the door. Everything was dark and
quiet. At least Rachel keeps the apartment
clean he thought, unlike that bitch Roxy. He
walked into the bedroom and saw Rachel
sleeping in a silk nightgown on their queen
size bed. Black Ice walked over to a floor
board in the closet and lifted it up. Inside
was some of the money he had stashed,
about $20,000, five ounces of crack, and 3
9mm guns. He took out some of the crack
jars from his pocket and put them with the
rest of the stash as well as the rest of the
money and guns he took from the two dead
men he killed earlier that day. He put the
guns, the chrome 38 revolver and the 22
caliber revolver, carefully aside the other
gun that was stashed. He covered it all back
with the wood floor board. He came out of
the closet and pulled his crack pipe out and
filled it up with crack and lit it. He inhaled
holding it in and then exhaled. He refilled
the glass pipe with more crack and did the
same. He repeated this taking three more
hits of the pipe until his eyes popped wide
open and felt revived with a bunch of

energy. His dick grew hard. He looked down at Rachel's sexy body with her dark brown skin complexion, lying on her side. Her ass was poking out of the sheets. He undressed and laid down on his side right beside Rachel. Then spit on his hand and rubbed it on his nine inch dick making it nice and wet for Rachel. He moved in closer to Rachel positioning his arm under and around her neck. He moved her panties to the side and rubbed his dick on her clit. He couldn't deal with no more foreplay he just rammed his dick insider her. "Ahhh," Rachel let out a moan while his dick penetrated hard and deep inside her. Black Ice started humping her in and out giving her all of him. "Ahhh, ohhh," Rachel moaned and began to arch her back poking her ass out even more. Even knowing Rachel hated that Black Ice beat her and her son and mistreated her, she loved him. She loved the feeling of his big black dick inside of her. "Mmmm, yes, yes baby, "Rachel moaned as Black Ice pulled her closer and tightening his arm around her neck. The crack had his dick hard as a rock. He raised Rachel's legs in the air while fucking her from the side and pounding away. "This is my wet pussy! Mine!" he moaned with each stroke going deeper and deeper inside her feeling her ass smack against his thighs and his balls, driving him even wilder. "Yes, yes baby," Rachel moaned.

Michael stood his six year old frame by his mother's door and watched his mother's legs were up in the air. He watched his father pound away on her. He had heard his mother screaming from his room and ran to her door to protect her from whatever she was screaming about. When he saw what she was hollering about, he just stood by the door mesmerized and just watched. He told himself he would kill his daddy if he hurt his mommy. Then Rachel moaned again, "Ahhhh," she opened her eyes and glanced over at the door to see her son standing there watching.

"Black Ice stop" Rachel said to Black Ice. He was too busy pounding away trying to get control over the nut that was about to explode deep inside her. He felt Rachel trying to move so he squeezed his arm that he had around her neck even tighter and gave her hard, long strokes not realizing that Michael was the reason of Rachel's attempt to stop fucking.

"Let go of my mommy!" Michael screamed while running over to the bed.

Black Ice looked over at his son while still humping Rachel's warm, wet pussy. He came all inside of her with one last hard stroke. He pulled out of her and jumped up out of the bed. He stood there with his black, naked shining body dripping with sweat. "Boy, take your little ass back in your bedroom!" he yelled at Michael.

"Don't hurt my mommy!" Michael yelled back.

Black Ice raised his hand and pulled it back and came down smacking Michael in the face. "Ahh," he cried as Michael hit the floor.

"Now, take your ass back into your bedroom!"

Michael got off the floor and wiped his tears with his little hands and stared into his father's eyes with an evil glare. Black Ice looked in his son's eyes and saw the evil inside them. He matched his stare. "Whenever you feel you're old enough and ready to take me, make your move punk! I'll be waiting." Black Ice warned Michael. "Now, get your little ass out of here".

Michael didn't move he just stood there staring into his father's eyes with an even more evil stare that overcame his face also. Rachel saw Black Ice raise his arm again knowing that he was going to strike Michael if she didn't do anything.

"I'm okay baby," Rachel hollered at Michael from the bed to prevent Black Ice from hitting her son. "Mommy is okay. Michael, please go back into your bedroom sweetie like you were told to do."

Michael looked at his mother's eyes to see if what she was telling him was the truth about her being okay. Once he saw what he needed to see, he turned toward his father and stared at him one last time before he walked out of the bedroom to go back to his own. Black Ice walked his naked body over to the dresser and picked up his glass pipe and stuffed it full of crack again. He held the lighter up to the pipe and inhaled and held it in and then exhaled. He wanted to take another hit, but the glass pipe got so hot it started to burn his hand when he was trying to light it. He put it down on the dresser. "Rachel, that little nigga is getting to grown. He's going to make me seriously hurt his little ass one day."

"He is your son Black Ice. Don't talk like that. He's just trying to protect me. Isn't that what you would want him to do if someone was hurting me?" Rachel asked.

"Yea, but not protect you from me.

You should have seen how that little fucker was looking at me. I'm the man in this house and I'll beat him and you when I see it necessary to do so."

Rachel hated when Black Ice started talking like that. He wasn't always like this that's what she fell in love with. She just wanted that man back and not this man that he is when he smokes that stuff. She could remember when they first met.

She lived on Saratoga Avenue in Brownsville on a side block in a house with her grandmother. Rachel never knew who her father was and her mother was always getting high on dope herself. She dropped Rachel off at her grandmother's house when she was five. Her grandmother was a fat, light skin woman. They called her, Momma. She had six kids of her own and they all grew up to run the streets. They came back too, but only to drop their own kids off to Momma and left it up to her to raise them. Momma's house was full with Rachel and her ten cousins. There were four girls and six boys all of different ages. Momma's youngest son, Brian, was still living in the house too. The house was filthy dirty. It was never picked up with dirty clothes scattered all over, garbage bags full of trash and kept just anywhere in the house making the house smell like a dump. It also smelled of urine and feces. There wasn't plumbing in the house. Everyone that had to use the restroom, had to use a bucket and when finished to throw the waste out in the back yard. But, a lot of the times, the buckets just stood where it was last used. Because of the waste smell in the house, it brought flies around the place.

Rachel had to share clothes with the other girl cousins, even underwear. The clothes were hardly ever laundered and freshly cleaned. There was never enough food in the house to feed everyone. Momma was taking the food stamps that she was receiving from welfare for all the kids and selling them for cash. She would leave and got to Atlantic City leaving the kids with her son Brian to watch while she stayed away for days. By the time she came home, she was broke. Rachel learned to take care of herself. She cleaned the house the best that she could and washed the little clothes that they had in the bathtub.

When Rachel turned fifteen, she was coming home from school. She was walking down the street daydreaming about getting out of Momma's house. Not paying any attention to her surroundings, she bumped into Black Ice. "Oh, I'm sorry." Rachel said as she looked up into the dark black skin, handsome face.

"There's nothing to be sorry about. You just bumped into me." He said back to Rachel with a big smile on his face. Rachel thought he had the most beautiful smell in the world and he was well dressed. Everything on him looked brand new.

"Where are you going?" Black Ice asked.

"I'm going home." She answered.

"Can I walk with you?"

"If you want to" Rachel replied with a smile, not use to the attention from such an attractive man. Rachel was a beautiful young woman with honey brown skin and an hour glass body shape. All the guys her age and older looked past her because she didn't dress like the other girls. It's not that she didn't want to. It was because she could not afford it.

"So, what's your name?" Black Ice asked her.

"It's Rachel, and yours?"

"Black Ice" Rachel looked up at him like he was crazy.

"I know your mother did not name

you Black Ice. So, what's your real name?"

"It's Michael Ice."

"I like that name, Michael."

"So Rachel how old are you?"

"I'm fifteen and you?"

"Twenty-one, do you have a boyfriend?"

"No, why do you want to be my boyfriend?"

"No." Black Ice said. Rachel looked at him with shock. "But, I do want to be your man." He pulled her to him and kissed her on the lips.

After that day, they were inseparable. Rachel fell head over heels in love with Black Ice. He bought her brand new clothes, but made her keep them at his apartment. He gave her money and anything that she needed or wanted. Black Ice thought this was his opportunity to mold Rachel into the perfect woman for himself. With Rachel being so young and innocent, he would be her first at everything.

A month after they had been together, Rachel was in Black Ice's apartment counting his drug money for him and putting it neatly into stacks for him. Black Ice grabbed her hands and led her into the bedroom. They kissed long and passionately. He took off her shirt and took off her bra to let her young firm breasts free. He slowly started sucking her nipples and licked around them. His had moved down to take off her jeans. Rachel got scared. They had fooled around before, but they never went all the way. She was still a virgin. "Black Ice, stop please." She said.

"Listen, Rachel, don't I take care of you? Now, if you want to continue to be my girl. You have to grow up and go through with this."

"But, I'm scared".

"There's nothing to be scared of I'll go slow" Black Ice again began to kiss her again and slowly pulled her jeans off her. He grabbed her ass and squeezed. He laid her down on the bed. As he removed his clothing until he was standing there naked, Rachel watched her man trusting every move he was going to make. He looked down at Rachel with his dick in his hand knowing that he was going to be taking Rachel's virginity. Her first like he wanted.

He climbed on the bed and on top of Rachel. He sucked her tits one by one and slid her panties off of her as he kissed and licked her thighs. He spread her legs as Rachel nervously opened up for him. He rubbed his dick on her pussy and gently tried to push his dick insider her. "Aaawww, it's too big. It won't fit." Rachel gasped.

"Hold on, baby" Black Ice got off the bed and went into the bathroom and returned with a bottle of baby oil. He poured a handful of the oil into his hand and rubbed it on to his dick making it nice and oily. He rubbed some on Rachel's pussy with his fingers. He climbed back into the bed and got on top of Rachel.

Rachel spread her legs again thinking he wasn't going to be able to get inside her. He was just too big for her virgin pussy. Black Ice leaned down and kissed her on the mouth and with one push slide into her. "Oh my God!" Rachel screamed.

"Relax and let me do me, ok," Black Ice said feeling Rachel's virgin pussy tight around his dick. She shook her head up and down nodding yes. Black Ice began to hump and grind in and out of her tight pussy. Rachel wrapped her arms around his back because it hurt with every stroke he made doing the best she could to take her mind off the pain. Black Ice kept humping and pumping away turning each stroke of pain into pleasure. She scratched into Black Ice's back while starting to enjoy the sweet sensation she was feeling inside of her. The penetration went deeper and deeper and then harder and harder. "Oh my god, oh my god" she yells as her body quivered uncontrollably as she came feeling like she was coming out of her body. Black Ice humped her as hard as he could and came inside of Rachel and collapsed on top of her.

"Damn, that pussy is good girl." Black Ice pulled out to see that his dick was covered with blood and cum.

"Oh my god, is that supposed to be there? Am I supposed to bleed like that?" Rachel asked.

"Yes, baby, it's okay. It's supposed to be there when it's your first time."

"It hurt at first, but started to feel good." Rachel told him.

They changed the sheets on the bed and jumped into the shower together.

After that day, Rachel was hooked to Black Ice. She would sneak out of momma's house at all times of the night, just to get some of Black Ice's sweet loving.

One morning, Rachel started throwing up. Every time she tried to eat something, she couldn't keep anything down. Rachel was so scared. She didn't know what to do or what was wrong with her. She walked to

the hospital to get checked out. They took a
urine sample and a blood test. She waited in
the waiting room for the results.

"Miss Rachel." A doctor called her
name out.

"Yes, that's me." Rachel said as she
stood up and walked towards him. She
followed him through the door and into a
patient room. "Please, have a seat young
lady." He said.

Rachel sat down in the chair. "Am I
going to die?" she asked the doctor. She
was scared she might have AIDS or an STD
like she had heard people talk about. She
and Black Ice were having unprotected sex
for a while now.

"No Miss Rachel. You're not going to
die, but you are going to be a mother.

"What?" Rachel exclaimed in a high
pitched voice.

"You are six weeks pregnant. Now, I
can't tell you what to do as far as to keep the
baby or not, but I can provide you with
information at make sure you have a healthy
baby."

The doctor gave Rachel the pamphlets
and information. She got up and left the
hospital. She started crying thinking she
was only fifteen years old. How could she

be a good mother? What was Black Ice going to say? What if he doesn't want the baby or her, then what? Rachel sat on the front porch stairs of momma's house and cried hysterically. She was supposed to meet Black Ice at this place, but didn't go.

When Rachel wasn't showing up at Black Ice's apartment, he got up and went out to look for Rachel. He knew it wasn't like her to not come when he told her to. He found Rachel sitting on the front porch stair's crying. "What's wrong, boo? Why didn't you come to my place when I asked you to do so? He asked Rachel.

Rachel didn't say anything. She just sat there and cried even harder. "Listen, talk to me. If there's a problem, we can fix it." Black Ice had started falling in love with Rachel. She would be the perfect wife for him in his eyes, because he had the chance to raise her and she did whatever he asked her to do.

"I didn't come to your place; because I was afraid you would hate me or leave me." Rachel said in tears.

"Rachel, I will never leave you and you will never leave me."

"Michael!" Rachel said aloud. Black Ice knew it was serious because Rachel never called him by his real name. He warned her never to do so. The streets know him as Black Ice and he couldn't afford for anyone on the streets to know his real name, just in case they wanted to start talking to the police about the things he did and things people thought he did, but nobody had any proof to prove it.

"Michael, I'm pregnant." Rachel finally let out.

A smile spread across his face. "I'm going to be a daddy?" Black Ice asked. Rachel nodded. He knew now he would have Rachel for life. Rachel was surprised at how well Black Ice took the news. He took her shopping and bought baby clothes, baby furniture, anything that they needed for their baby to come. He fixed up one of the bedrooms into a nursery with baby things and a crib. He fed Rachel with her favorite foods, rubbed her belly and oiled it down for her. Rachel was falling deeply in love with him. Rachel felt like the luckiest woman alive. She still lived at momma's house, but once her grandmother found out that she was pregnant she'd kick her out, like she did with her own kids. Rachel knew she'd go and live with Black Ice and that would make her really happy. He already wanted her to stay with him, but she wanted to leave things with momma on a good note.

Rachel was sleeping in a nightgown and rubbed her belly in the room that she had to share with one of her girl cousins that was thirteen. Momma's youngest son, Brian was twenty-one years old; he was sitting on the floor naked in the closet waiting for the girls to go to sleep. Once he was sure they were asleep, he would creep out and slowly get on top of Rachel. Rachel felt a hand on her mouth and the weight of a man on top of her. When she opened her eyes, she was shocked to see her uncle naked on top of her with a knife to her neck. "What are you doing?" Rachel asked. He threw his hand over her mouth to keep her quiet. "Shut the fuck up! If you say another fucking word, I swear I'll cut you!" Briand said as he looked her in her eyes. With Brian's free hand, he lifted up her nightgown and ripped her panties off of her. He stuck his two fingers inside of her. Tears started to roll down Rachel's face. She couldn't believe what was happening to her. Out of all the people in the world, she was being raped by her own uncle. "Stop!" Rachel screamed.

Brian forced his hand down on her mouth as hard as he could and cut her on the side of the neck. "Didn't I tell you to shut the fuck up, bitch?" Rachel screamed in pain from the cut on her neck, but the hand that covered her mouth let no sound escape for anyone to hear. Brian shoved his dick inside of Rachel.

"You bitch!" he said as he started to fuck her. "Give me this pussy. I hear you out there fucking. It's about time I get a piece of this ass!"

All Rachel could do was just lie there and cry as her uncle's dick went in and out of her. She wanted to scream for help, but was too scared that he would kill her. She felt the sharp knife up against her neck. She felt the blood running down her neck from where he cut her.

"Yes, yes, bitch. You're lucky I have been fucking your other cousin. I have been waiting to get your ass, but you're always sneaking out to that nigga's crib." He said as he was squeezing Rachel's sore breasts. He pulled up her nightgown even higher and sucked on her nipples. "Mmm, yes, yes" Brian was feeling the nut building up. So he pounded and pounded away holding on to Rachel's mouth. Rachel turned her head. She didn't want to look him in his eyes or see his face. The tears kept coming down from her eyes. She glanced at her little cousin in the other bed, who was fast asleep not hearing a sound that was happening in the same room.

Her cousin, Janet, wasn't sleeping. She was lying down on the pillow, but with her eyes wide open crying. She watched her uncle hump her cousin Rachel as he was moaning on top of her.

When Brian came, he climbed off Rachel. "If you open your mouth about this, bitch, I will do more than just cut you. I'll put this knife up your pussy." Brian said and meant every word. He walked his naked body out of the bedroom. Rachel started to cry uncontrollably. She couldn't understand why this was happening to her. Her younger cousin got out of her bed and came over to hug Rachel. "Rachel, don't cry. He's a monster. De does this to all of us."

"What?" Rachel asked. "Did he rape you too?

"Yes," Janet answered with tears coming down her face. "He does much worse things to me. He's done this to every girl in this house, our ten year old cousin and even the eight year old. I tried to tell Momma, but she won't believe me. He

51

found out I told Momma and came in here on one of those nights you sneaked out to see Black Ice and he put his penis in my butt and took that knife he always carries, and put it inside of me" Janet said while crying.

"What do you mean he put it inside of you?" Rachel asked.

"He will do what he told you he'd do, if you tell anyone. He rammed it into my pussy cutting me up. I bled for two weeks. Momma thought I was out there messing around with some boy and said it was my own fault."

Rachel stopped crying and sat up on her bed and held her cousin. Rachel's pain felt little compared to what her little cousin had been through. Both girls cried the night away in each other's arms.

It was five o'clock in the morning; Rachel was still up holding her cousin in her arms who was fast asleep. Rachel carefully moved her arms and laid her cousin down on the pillow. Rachel got up and got dressed and walked out of the house. She headed over to Black Ice's apartment.

She knocked on the door. Black Ice heard the knocking at this door and wondered who the hell would be knocking at his door so early. He grabbed his 44 calico-revolver from the nightstand drawer and went to open the door to see Rachel. Rachel looked at Black Ice with nothing on, but his boxer's and a gun in his hand.

"Girl, what's wrong with you knocking on my door so early. I thought you were a stick up or the cops." Rachel didn't say anything. Black Ice saw the tears still in her eyes. Then he saw how red her face was and could tell she had been crying for a long time. "Baby, what's wrong? Come in." He said as he led her through the door. She sat down on the couch with tears again starting to roll down her face. Black Ice sat down next to her and noticed the cut on her neck. "Yo, who did that to you?" Black Ice asked with anger in his voice.

Rachel wiped her tears off her face. "My, my uncle raped me tonight and cut me with a knife. He said that he'd do worse to me if I told somebody."

"What?" Black Ice said with anger and frustration coming over his face. He quickly got dressed and put the 44 calico-revolver in his waistband. "Yo, does he ever leave the house?"

"Yes, he leaves at six in the morning every day to go to the store to buy a pack of cigarettes."

"Come on, Rachel" He said as he grabbed her hands.

"Where are we going?" she asked.

"I want you to point him out to me."

"Why? You can't do anything to him. He will hurt me and my little cousins more than he has already. He told me not to tell anyone or he would do worse than he has already."

A few minutes later, Rachel and Black Ice were on the corner of Saratoga Avenue sitting in the car. "If he goes to the store, he will have to pass by this corner. The store is on the next block." Black Ice said to aloud to no one in particular. Black Ice and Rachel patiently waited on the corner of the block. She couldn't understand why they were there though. No sooner that she that thought crossed her mind, she saw her Uncle Brian walking towards them. "That's him." Rachel said pointing towards him.

"Oh, I'll let him get closer." Black Ice said when he saw Brian. He got out of the car. Black Ice was standing on the side of a building waiting for Brian to get closer to him. When Brian appeared in his vision, Black Ice popped out from the side of the wall behind him. Brian was still walking unaware of Black Ice's presence behind him.

"Yo! Yo! Brian!"

Brian turned around to see who was calling his name. AS soon as he turned his head, he instantly saw nothing but stars. Black Ice struck him in his head with the butt of the 44 calico-revolver. Brian tried to open his eyes to see who hit him. When his eyes finally were able to focus again, he was struck with the barrel of the gun to his face. "Yo what do you want?" Brain asked.

"Go into that alley way." Black Ice ordered.

"What for?"

"If you don't go, I'm going to blow your fucking brains out, right here, right now."

"Alright" Brian said as he walked in to the alley way and was surprised to see Rachel standing right there. "What the fuck is this?"

"Don't play stupid, nigga. You raped my woman."

Brian turned around to face Black Ice, "Fuck you and your bitch! The pussy was good. What you going to do nigga, shoot me? I bet if you put that gun down I'd whip your ass." Brian said.

"Oh yea" Black Ice put the gun back in his waist band and covered it up with his shirt.

"Black Ice, please let's just go."
Rachel said.

"Step back, Rachel. And let me
handle this." Black Ice said staring at Brian.

"Yea, bitch shut up! Let this pussy
handle his business. After I fuck him up,
I'm going to fuck him too. Then I'm going
to stab the both of you mother fuckers!"
Brian hollered.

Just as Brian said the last word that
came out of his mouth, Black Ice punched
him in the jaw and jabbed him in the nose.
Brian stumbled backwards. Brian pulled out
a five inch knife that curved at the tip. He
started swinging it at Black Ice. He moved
to the side and dodged the knives pathway.
Brian came towards Black Ice with the blade
pointed at him trying to run it in him. Black
Ice punched Brian in the eye slowing down
his attack. Black Ice grabbed Brian's hand
that had the knife and twisted his arm back.
Brian hollered and dropped the knife to the
ground. Black Ice twisted harder until he
heard a popping sound. He knew he broke
his arm. He released his grip and Brian
went to his knees crying holding on to his
arm. "You son of a bitch, you broke my
fucking arm!"

Brian tried to reach for the knife on the ground, but he only got kicked in his face before he got close to it. Rachel stood back watching the whole thing in shock, not knowing what to do. Brian stood up and Black Ice clinched his hand around his throat. Brian gasped for air. He tried to punch black Ice in the face, but it had no effect on him. Black Ice gripped tighter on his throat and he squeezed Brian's wind pipe until his sharp fingernails pierced his flesh. Brian squirmed and did his best to get free from Black Ice. Black Ice outweighed him with his brutal strength. Brian saw the rage in Black Ice's eyes and felt his body get weaker. He continued to slowly try to swing at Black Ice in the face, but with each swing he made the hits became lighter. Black Ice kept squeezing tighter and locked down on his wind pipe. With all his strength, the flesh from Brian's neck started to tear and rip apart. Black Ice pulled with all his might and ripped away the flesh he had locked in his hand. A big whole opened up on Brian's neck and blood poured out as Brian fell to the ground.

"Oh my God!" Rachel screamed.

"Shut up, Rachel!" Black Ice yelled at her.

She walked over to Black Ice and her uncle's body that was squirming and flopping around on the ground. Then there was no movement at all. Rachel reached for Black Ice's hands. She looked to see the blood and what he still had holding in his hand. He opened his hands to let her see. Rachel couldn't believe what her eyes had seen. Black Ice had a piece of her uncle's wind pipe. "You ripped out his wind pipe?" Rachel screamed. Black Ice gave her an evil eye. He got up and put the piece of flesh in his pocket. He picked up the knife that Brian dropped to the ground.

"What are you doing?" Rachel asked.

"Didn't I tell you to shut up?" Black Ice said. Rachel looked in his eyes and saw nothing but evil in them. Black Ice pulled down Brian's jeans and then his boxers. He took the knife and grabbed his dick and started sawing away at it. Rachel screamed at what she saw. She heard people in the neighborhood talk about how evil and cold hearted Black Ice was, but she never believed them. Now, with her own eyes she saw him kill someone without breaking a sweat and doing monstrous things to the dead body.

Rachel threw up in the alley way.

When Black Ice detached Brian's dick from his dead body, he took it and stuffed it in Brian's mouth. "Talk shit now, punk!"

Black Ice grabbed Rachel even though she was still throwing up and pulled her out of the alley way. He took her back to the car and drove back to his apartment. That was Rachel's first time seeing him kill someone, but she knew in her heart it wasn't the first time.

"Rachel, you can't ever go back and live with Momma. You go back and tell her that you're pregnant and you are going to live with me."

"Okay." Rachel said sick to her stomach and crying.

"Why the fuck are you crying? I know you aren't crying over that rapist uncle of yours."

"No, but why did you kill him? I never seen anybody get killed before."

"Listen Rachel, I don't want you to ever bring this shit up again. I killed him because he touched what is mines and no one touches what is mines."

From that day on, Rachel stayed with Black Ice. Everything was what she dreamed of. They made love every night and day. He wined and dined her. He took her to all of her doctor's appointments to check on their baby growing inside her.

When Rachel gave birth to a baby boy, she named him Michael Junior, after his father. After the birth of her son, was when the abuse started. Black Ice wouldn't let her leave the apartment and became very possessive of her. He'd beat Rachel for everything and anything. Even if the baby would cry, he would beat her. Rachel learned the hard way while the streets called Michael Sr., Black Ice. Rachel stepped back into reality and watched Black Ice naked body for the back. He was standing at the dresser with sweat running down his back and the glass crack pipe in his mouth. She continued to watch as he inhaled the crack smoke again and again. Rachel covered her face thinking it always wasn't like this.

Chapter 8

"Bitch, take this dick. Whose pussy is this?"

"This pussy is yours. Mmm, yes daddy. Fuck me, fuck me, yes." Lisa moaned. "Fuck me, Caesar."

Caesar pounded away on Lisa's pussy from the back. He smacked her ass and watched it shake while giving long hard strokes up inside Lisa. "I'm about to cum." He yelled as he squeezed her ass even tighter and pounded even faster and harder.

When he came, he felt his body go weak and his dick going limp. He collapsed down on the bed and Lisa did the same lying right next to him. Both of their bodies were covered in sweat and weak from fucking. "Damn, baby that felt so good." Lisa said out of breath.

"I'll bet he don't fuck you like that. Does he?" Caesar asked.

"No, daddy, only you put it on me like that. He can't go that long or that deep." Lisa said to Caesar about Ace.

Lisa and Caesar busted out laughing. "Yo, how's Mark?" Caesar asked.

"He's fine baby. I gave him the new clothes you got for him."

"I don't know how Ace can't tell that's not his kid." Caesar said to Lisa. "Mark looks just like me."

"Nigga please, I have that nigga so pussy whipped. He doesn't know left from right." Lisa said while giggling.

"Have you been getting in his head about Black Ice.? I need him with me if we're going to take out Black Ice's business."

"Yes, I been fucking with him and pushing his buttons. He's with it. He scared some nigga with more money is going to come along and take me away from him.

Caesar smiled, "Too bad he don't know a nigga already took you without him knowing. But on the real, boo. Keep getting into his head and make sure he stays down with the plan and after we take over. I'm going to take you away from that lame ass nigga and make you mine."

"Oh daddy," Lisa replied. She licked her lips and grabbed his dick and slit it into her wet, warm mouth.

"Mmmm, yeah girl, suck that shit." Caesar said. Lisa used her tongue and licked around the head of his dick. She used moved her tongue to make her way down to his balls and took each, one by one, and

sucked on them. "Ahhh shit, yes baby."
Caesar said while clenching his teeth. Lisa
took both of his balls in her mouth and
sucked them at the same time. "Damn girl."
She made her way back to the head of his
dick and worked away at it.

As Lisa worked her magic, Caesar
thought to himself, everything is going as
planned. Caesar has been fucking Lisa for
three years now. Ace warned him when they
first got together not to fuck with Lisa on
that level. Everybody knows the saying
'You can't turn a whore in to a housewife'.
Lisa was a whore in its true form. She had
fucked every nigga in Brownsville projects.
Then Ace came along and made her his girl
and got her pregnant. He moved her out of
the projects.

No soon after Lisa had the baby,
Caesar found her cheating on Ace with some
dude from the Bronx. She was giving him
head in the backseat of his car. Lisa had
seen Caesar's care roll by and knew he saw
her. She knew that she fucked up. She
didn't want to lose the meal ticket with Ace.
So, Lisa put that magic dick suck game on
Caesar. Since then, they were fucking ever
since. He started fucking her raw and she
ended up pregnant with Caesar's baby.

Being the true scandalous chick she was, she lied and told Ace it was his baby. And she still kept Caesar on the side so she could have her cake and eat it too.

Caesar let out a loud moan as he busted a nut in Lisa's mouth. "Swallow every drip of my cum and lick it off my dick." Caesar smiled to himself. He thought no way in hell was he going to take this scandalous bitch from Ace and take care of her. If she cheats on her man, she will damn sure do the same to him. When he takes over Black Ices' drug business, he will take his son, Mark, from her and raise his son himself. But, before he leaves her ass to fend for herself, he will use Lisa to keep Ace from backing out on him. He will just keep enjoying the good ass head she be giving to him.

Chapter 9

Black Ice was furious. It's been months and he still hasn't heard a word from Roxy. She had run away when he was gone the day after he found her fucking those two guys that he killed. Every day that went by and he couldn't find her, the angrier he got. It showed he took it out on Rachel. "Bitch, I told you to smoke this shit!"

"No I won't." Black Ice punched her in the nose that sent her flying back. Rachel punched him back, but her hit did little to nothing to him. Black Ice punched her again and again until Rachel fell to the floor. She curled up into a ball, covering herself. Michael Jr. watched as his father repeatedly kicked his mother on the floor over and over again. Tears rolled down his little face. He cried for the beating his mother was getting. Michael cried out as his father bent down to stop hurting his mother. But his father just bent down and continued to punch Rachel in the head.

Michael couldn't understand why his father hit his mother and beat her to bad that it left marks on her body. It always left his mother crying for days. She would even cry on days that she didn't get beat by him.

Michael knew why thought. He knew that
his mother would be thinking the same thing
that he did. Why did his father always hit
her? He hollered at his father, "Daddy,
daddy, stop!" Michael couldn't let him
continue to hit his mother. He knew that he
couldn't stop his father, but that wouldn't
stop him from trying to help her. Michael
ran toward his father in hopes of biting him
in the leg again. Black Ice turned around
and saw his son running towards him. One
quick move, he back handed Michael upside
the head. "Your little ass wants some, I'll
give you some," Black Ice said. He walked
over to his son and smacked him again.
Rachel glanced to see her son on the floor
crying and getting beat by his father. She
used the little strength she had left and got
up. She rand and jumped on Black Ice's
back and wrapped her arms around his neck.
"Stop hitting my son, you bastard! I'll kill
you myself. Leave my baby alone."

Rachel's grip tightened around his
neck causing Black Ice to squirm around to
try and shake her off him. But, he couldn't.
He usually overpowered Rachel's defenses.
Since Black Ice had been smoking crack, he
lost a lot of weight. His 220 frame went
down to 50 and his wife almost weighed

more than him now. "Get off me, bitch."
Black Ice leaned his back over flipping
Rachel off him. He went to the living room
where the TV was and pulled the extension
cord from the wall and wrapped it around
his hand.

"I'll teach you two to try and jump
me." He swung down hitting Michael with
the extension cord across his face. Then he
hit Rachel. Rachel crawled over to her son
and used her body to shield her son from
Black Ice.

"You both are stupid mother fuckers.
I run this house!" Black Ice yelled. Rachel
and Michael cried while both trying to take
the beating for each other. Black Ice kept
swinging the extension cord beating his wife
and son until he was out of breath. "That
should teach you the next time you all try
some shit like that again. The next time will
be worse." He said as he walked away
leaving the apartment.

Black Ice left his wife and son crying
and bleeding. They were covered with welts
to their skin.

"See mommy. I won't let you get
beat by yourself. We'll get beat together."
Michael said to his mother.

Rachel lay on the floor holding her

son. It took her a minute to clearly understand what her son had just said to her, but once she did, she cried uncontrollably. She understood now that all this abuse was traumatizing her baby. Michael looked up from under his mother's arms to see her crying even harder. "Mommy, don't cry. I love you. Please don't cry. I'll always take the beatings with you." Michael started crying seeing his mother cry. They lay on the floor holding each other and cried their pains away.

Chapter 10

Black Ice pulled his Lexus ES slowly in front of the Brownsville Projects on Mother Gaston Avenue. He watched Ace and Caesar running the block with the workers. Black Ice rolled down his passenger window, "Yo, jump the fuck in."

Ace and Caesar got in the back seat of the car. "Where's my money?" Black Ice demanded while holding his 44 calico-revolver in his lap.

"I got three thousand for you, here." Caesar said and passed him the bundle of money.

"Yo, I got two thousand for you." Ace replied while handing him the money.

"Yo, where the fuck is the rest of it?"

"Yo, Black Ice we gave you the rest of it yesterday. I gave you 3 G and Ace gave you 4 G. You don't remember?" Caesar answered.

Black Ice raised his gun and pointed it in Caesar's face. "Nigga, you better not be playing with my money. I think you're playing with my money." Black Ice said devilishly.

Caesar looked in his eyes and knew he just saw the devil. "Black Ice, I'm telling you, boss we gave you everything yesterday."

"I know, fool. I'm just testing you." Black Ice replied while putting his gun back on his lap. Before Black Ice pulled away he handed Caesar twelve ounces a piece to bag up. Caesar and Ace go out of the car and Black Ice drove off.

They walked over to Caesar's car, an Acura Legend and got in. Ace leaned in the driver side window to talk to Caesar. "Yo, you see what I mean that nigga smoking to much of that shit. He almost killed our ass for thinking we didn't pay him."

"Yeah, you're right. That nigga is tripping, but what we supposed to do?" Ace asked.

"Yo, I have a plan." Caesar replied. "Hop in."

"Hold on let me put this work in my car." Ace walked down to his car and opened up the trunk and put the twelve ounces in it and locked it. He came back and hopped in the passenger seat and shut the door. "So, what's your plan?"

"Yo, you know J-Rock, that nigga on Pitkin Avenue?" Caesar said.

"Yea, J-Rock has a team over there selling drugs there doing, but they aren't making more money than us." Ace replied.

"Well, listen, I'm going to see if I can get J-Rock to handle Black Ice for us."

"Man your crazy. You know that nigga is scared to death of Black Ice. No one in their right mind around here would fuck with him."

"Listen, you got to stop thinking like that. Don't you need more money for Lisa and the kids?" Caesar asked. As soon as Caesar said that, Ace tensed up. He'll do anything for her and hated when a nigga acted like he wouldn't.

"Yo, don't even bring Lisa and the kids name into this. Yes, I'm down. Let's roll and find J-Rock."

"Alright, that's what I'm talking about." Caesar said and started the car and pulled off. He knew by saying Lisa's name it would get Ace down with him. It was a low blow, but he had to push his buttons. He needed Ace's help to run the business for a while, because he didn't trust the young boys on the block to do so. But as soon as he found a nigga he could trust, he planned on killing Ace too. Caesar drove three blocks over and made a right and pulled in front of a building with young thugs hanging out in front of it selling crack. One of the boys was named Smoke. He was a tall slim cat who was only eighteen and ran the block for J-Rock. Smoke walked over to Caesar's car window, "Yo what's up? What you all doing over here. We don't have any problems with you." Smoke said while his hand rested on the gun in his waist band. He wanted no problems with Caesar and Ace, not so much as them. He could care less about killing them. He'll put a bullet in their heads in a heartbeat, but it was Black Ice he feared. Shit the whole hood feared that crazy nigga. But, Caesar and Ace were part of his team and there would be hell to pay if someone killed them. Smoke wasn't about to let a nigga come over and shoot him down like a dog. A man is a man, no matter what.

"Yo, go get J-Rock for me and tell him I need to talk to him." Caesar said while hanging out of the window of his car. He used the door to cover the cocked 9mm pistol in his hand.

"Alright I'll go see if he wants to talk to you." Smoke replied while walking off and entering the building where all the young hustlers were at. All of their eyes glanced over on Caesar's car. The young hustlers were leery of them. Caesar never

72

really like Smoke and he was another nigga on his list to kill when he made it to the top.

A middle built brown skin man came out of the building followed by Smoke and walked up to the car. "Yo, hop in the back seat, you and Smoke." Caesar said. J-Rock looked nervously and wondered if he should be getting in the car with Caesar and Ace.

"Yo, I'm not going to pull off. We can stay right in front of your building." Caesar said. J-Rock hesitated and hopped in with Smoke. They were strapped so he was a feeling a little safer. J-Rock thought you could never just trust any nigga in the hood, especially a nigga that is crazy enough to run with Black Ice. "So, what the two of you want to talk to us about?" J-Rock asked with an attitude.

"Listen, I know you want to make some more money than what your pulling on this little ass block. So, Ace and I have a deal for you."

"Ok, what kind of deal?" J-Rock asked listening with all ears. The talk of money always got his attention. Caesar smiled then looked at Ace sitting in the passenger seat.

"It's like this. Black Ice is falling off.

73

That nigga is smoking crack hard and he's losing his damn mind, whatever he had to begin with. He's losing a lot of his body weight." Caesar started explaining some stuff first.

"Yeah, I heard that nigga is smoking that shit now. And he is looking kind of fucked up. But, what's the point?" J-Rock asked.

"My point is Ace and I will be taking over Black Ice's business."

"Yeah right, like Black Ice is just going to hand over his business." Smoke said butting in to the conversation.

"I was talking to J-Rock, not you Smoke and the words I used was take over. And how are we going to do that you wonder? We need you, J-Rock, and some of your men to kill him and in return we'll pay you fifteen thousand. Not only that we'll give you the day-shift to sell crack in the Brownsville Projects every other week."

"Nigga, are you crazy? Is this some trick or something?" J-Rock asked. "Black Ice will kill us all just for talking about this shit."

"Naw nigga, that mother fucker is too busy smoking crack and looking for that bitch, Roxy. We can pull this off. I'm serious." Caesar responded looking at J-Rock in his eyes. J-Rock knew then he was for real that this wasn't any kind of trick.

"Yo, you remember what happened to the last dude who tried to take over Black Ice's business? That nigga, Lip from Riverhead Projects, and his men killed five of Black Ice's workers. In return, Black Ice killed everybody. When he couldn't find Lip's ass, he kidnapped the nigga's grandmother and mother and put the word on the street that he would let them go if Lip gave himself up to him. That fool Lip gave himself up to Black Ice. Black Ice duck taped him to a chair in one of his apartments and shot the fools grandmother in front of him. Then he raped his mother in front of him and emptied a clip in her. That wasn't the worst part, Black Ice cut off both of Lip's hands, tied them together with a piece of rope, and threw them up on the telephone lines. The project kids thought they were a pair of sneakers and left them just hanging there. When the cops finally noticed the hands up there, they took them down. In the hand's there was a note that read,

"If you ever try and take what are mines, I'll take more than their hands."

A week later they found Lip's body,

75

but his head was gone. To this day, the cops have never found his head. Word on the street is Back Ice kept Lip's head in one of his apartments with the rest of the pieces of body parts he took off his victims."

"Listen I know the fucking story, J-Rock. Are you down or what? The nigga isn't the same. He's falling off from smoking that shit." Caesar said.

"So what, you think that makes him less dangerous or more?" Smoke asked.

"Fuck I'm down." J-Rock replied while thinking about all the money he'd make selling drugs in the projects. "So, what's the plan?"

"Let's give Black Ice another month and let him keep smoking himself to death. Then you and your men will come while Ace and I are talking business with him keeping him busy. So he won't see it coming or hear anything to react to it."

"Alright I'm cool with that, but let me ask y'all one thing." J-Rock said.

"What?" Caesar asked.

"Why don't the two of you just kill him yourself?"

"Because that nigga is high, but he's not stupid. He doesn't sleep on me and Ace."

"That's what I thought."

"Alright I'll get up with tow," Caesar said and pulled off. "You see how east that went Ace?"

"Yea, I see, but I hope we can pull everything off." Ace said.

"Don't hope nigga. WE will there's no room for doubt."

J-Rock and Smoke stood in front of their building watching Caesar's car make its way down the block.

"So, what you think, Smoke?" J-Rock asked.

"Shit I think these fools are crazy to want to cross Black Ice."

"Yea, but if there right about him slipping and falling off, I think we can kill him."

"Yea and then kill Caesar and Ace's ass and take over" Smoke snickered.

"The whole mother fucking strap for ourselves," J-Rock replied. "It sounds good to me. I never liked that pussy Caesar anyways. Cool let see how things fall out."

Chapter 11

Michael stood and watched his father sleep on the black living room couch. He was surprised to see his father sleeping. Something his father didn't do much of since he started smoking that funny smelling stuff. Michael looked down at his father's feet and saw the glass pipe and some empty small jars. He remembered seeing him one time take the white stuff out of the jars to smoke it. A devilish smile crossed Michael's face, he slowly crept over to where his father was sleeping and bent down and picked up the glass pipe and the four empty jars. He ran back into his bedroom. Ten minutes later, he came back into the living room and carefully placed the glass pipe back on the floor next to his father's feet.

Black Ice jumped up out of his sleep with a disgusted look on his face. He looked around the living room and saw Michael standing in front of him just staring at him. Michael gave Black Ice a sinister look. Chills went down Black Ice's back as he looked into his son's eyes. There wasn't much that scared Black Ice, but he could see complete evil in his son's eyes. The only time he ever saw a pair of eyes like that was when he looked in the mirror.

"Yo, what the fuck are you looking at? Go in your fucking room."

Michael just stood there and looked at Black Ice. When he was ready he turned around and walked away while giving him an evil glare.

Black Ice thought that he was going to have to kill that boy one day. He reached in his pocket and pulled out to small jars of crack. He looked around on the couch for his crack pipe. He noticed it was on the floor by his feet. He bent over and picked it up and stuffed the pipe full of crack. He took out his lighter and held it to the end of the pipe and inhaled deeply. As soon as he inhaled, he knew something was wrong. He could feel the inside of his throat being ripped to shreds. The feeling traveled down to his chest, then to his stomach. "Aw shit." Black Ice gasped as he repeatedly coughed trying to het air. He felt his insides ripping apart what felt like sand in his mouth. He started to cough up blood. He used his hand to cover his mouth to stop the blood from flying all over the place. He tried to focus his eyes and couldn't believe what he saw. He had coughed up little tiny pieces of glass.

"What the fuck?" Black Ice yelled out and coughed up more blood. He collapsed on the floor.

Rachel ran out of the bedroom and into the living room after hearing her man gasping for air. Rachel looked down and saw Black Ice on the floor covered in his own blood. He was still coughing up blood and holding his neck. "Oh my God baby what's wrong?" She bent down to help him and held his head in her lap. "Speak to me, what's wrong?" Rachel asked again with tears drawing up in her eyes.

Black Ice was unable to answer her. IT was too difficult for him to breathe and all he could do was cough up blood. Black Ice turned his head that was in Rachel's lap too see that his son was standing right there. Looking him in the eyes with an evil smile across his face. Black Ice coughed up more blood. "You little fucker" He coughed as the words slowly came out of his mouth before he passed out and his world went dark.

Michael watched with amazement as his father coughed up blood and passed out, but he couldn't understand why his mother was crying and trying to help him. "Mommy, don't cry it will be over soon just let him die."

"Shut up, shut up, Michael. You sound like your father." Rachel jumped up with tears running down her face and ran to the telephone and called 911.

Michael wondered why she was helping him after all the times he beat them. He did this for her. Earlier when his father was asleep and he took the glass pipe and the jars back into his bedroom, he put the jars into a sock and used his sneaker to crush and grind the glass into tiny little pieces. He stuffed the pieces into both ends of the glass pipe and placed it back on the floor next to his father's feet where he found it.

"Mommy, let him die."

"Stop fucking talking that way" Rachel demanded.

Michael never heard his mother cuss at him. So, he knew she was mad. He could see the tears in his mother's eyes and it made him cry. "I don't understand mommy." Still not comprehending why his mother still loved his father after all the beatings they received from him.

Chapter 12

Black Ice woke up in a panic. He could see where he was at. His throat and chest burned. He moved his hands to his face to feel tubes in his nose and mouth. He yanked them out. He yelled in pain. He looked around the room to notice he was in a hospital bed just as Rachel walked into the hospital room. She was followed in by a tall white man, a doctor. "Well I see you're up. That's great."

"What's going on?" Black Ice asked in a faint whisper. His throat was very sore.

"Mr. Ice we had to pump your stomach and throat. You had tiny pieces of glass that were ripping apart your insides. You're lucky your wife called 911 to get you to the hospital on time. If she would have waited any longer the glass would have cut your wind pipe so bad it would have stopped your breathing permanently. I'm not about to ask you how the glass got in your system, because I found traces of cocaine in your blood. Just be grateful to your wife." And with that being said, the doctor turned his back and walked out of the hospital room.

"Thank you, Doctor Paul" Rachel said.

"You're welcome young lady."

Rachel walked over to Black Ice's bed, "Baby, I'm happy to see that you're up. The doctor said you could leave in the morning." Rachel placed a kiss on his lips.

Black Ice looked at his woman in her eyes. Time's like these reminded him why he loved her so much. It didn't matter how much he beat her or mistreated her. She was always there for him, even more the reason why he's got to get her to smoke crack with him so he would never lose her. He felt that would keep her in his life forever. Little did he know Rachel would stay with him without being trapped for good or for bad, she just proved it by saving his life, but he was too blind to see it.

"Baby, how did you inhale all that glass?" she asked.

"I got an idea on how." Black Ice flashed back to the evil smile he saw on his son's face.

"Well, I hope you stop smoking that stuff and things will be different". Rachel said.

"Oh things will be different." He said in a sarcastic voice that Rachel didn't catch.

"I love you and I will see you when you come home." Rachel said while hugging and kissing him good-bye. She left the hospital praying that things would be different for her family. She hoped things would be different, but she just didn't know how.

Chapter 13

The next day, Black Ice left Brookdale Hospital. He walked up to the apartment and put the key in his door. When he walked in, he could see Rachel in the kitchen hot combing her hair. Once he reached the living room, he looked down to see Michael drawing a picture on the floor by the couch. Michael stopped drawing and glanced up at this father and went back to drawing his picture. Black Ice couldn't believe his eyes. His son just tried to kill him yesterday and didn't even break a sweat or look at all nervous when he saw him. Black Ice thought that little nigga is evil, but he knew he could only blame himself. It was his own blood that was flowing through his son's veins. But, then he thought fuck that, this little nigga tried to kill him and he was going to have to teach him a lesson. Black Ice walked back into the bedroom and returned with his leather belt wrapped in his hands. Rachel looked at the belt and knew what time it was. "What are you doing? You just came home from the hospital and you already want to start something." Rachel shouted.

"This has nothing to do with you."

Black Ice said as he walked towards his son.
Rachel jumped up from the kitchen chair
where she was hot combing her hair and ran
in between Black Ice and Michael with her
arms spread wide open trying to block his
way. "Rachel, I'm only going to tell you
once, move!" he yelled.
"What for?" she asked.
"This little nigga tried to kill me
yesterday. It was him who put that glass in
my pipe."
"How do you know that?"
"Because I do, now move"
"No, my son wouldn't have done
what you're accusing him of."
Michael looked up from the floor
where he was drawing and watched his
mother and father argue. He wished silently
that his father did die yesterday. Just then
Black Ice took the belt he had wrapped
around his hand and put it around Rachel's
neck to choke her. "Didn't I tell your ass to
move?" Black Ice said while clenching his
teeth. Rachel gasped for air and tried to
swing her arms to get free of his grip, but it
was no use. Black Ice squeezed tighter.
"Daddy stop, please, please stop!" Michael
cried. At the sight of his mother's arms
swinging around like a dead rag doll. Black

Ice's grip was too much. As Rachel fell to the floor passing out from the clench around her neck, she thought 'I gave him life and he is going to take mine away'.

Black Ice released his grip and watched Rachel body fall to the floor with dead weight. Michael crawled to his mother and put his hands on her face. "Mommy, mommy sit up" He cried. As soon as Michael said those words, he felt the belt go across his back.

"Your little ass wanted to try to kill me!" Black Ice questioned Michael as he repeatedly stuck his son with the belt across his little body. Michael cried and rolled up into a ball to try to protect himself. "Mommy, help me!" he cried.

"You little fucker, I'm going to teach you to cross me!" Black Ice yelled. He beat Michael for a half an hour. Leaving Michael on the floor crying and covered in blood and more welts added to the previous beatings.

Black Ice returned to the living room looking at his son and decided that he wasn't done with him. Black Ice walked in the kitchen looking for something else to beat his son with. He looked at the stove to see that Rachel left the hot comb on the oven. Black Ice grinned and grabbed the hot comb by its handle making sure not to touch the hot part. He walked back in the living room to his crying son and bent down and grabbed his left arm. Michael was to sore and weak to put up a fight. Black Ice placed the hot comb on Michael's arm. Michael screamed as loud as he could and tried to pull his arm away, but it was locked in his father's grip. The heat from the hot comb sizzled and cooked his flesh. It burned his skink deeply. Rachel regained consciousness when she heard the blood wrenching screams her son let out. She looked up to see that Black Ice was holding he hot comb and pressing against her son's arm. Rachel jumped up and pushed Black Ice with all the strength and energy she had. She made him fall over to the side. He released his grip from Michael's arm and dropped the hot comb to the floor. She jumped on top of Black Ice and punched away with everything she had left in her. "Don't touch my baby." She screamed while swinging wildly at his face.

Black Ice punched Rachel in the temple knocking her right off of him. He got up and started to kick her in the ribs. Black Ice was furious. While kicking Rachel, he wondered why he was having so many problems with his own family. He looked down and saw that she couldn't take any more. He knew she wouldn't be putting up a fight anymore. Black Ice picked up the hot comb for the floor and reached for Michael and again put in on Michael's skin. He grabbed his neck and started choking him. Tears were still running down Michael's face as Black Ice moved the hot comb towards his face. "Mommy," Michael said in a pleaded whisper. He couldn't get all the words out as the grip around his neck grew tighter.

"No! Stop please. Don't burn him anymore!" Rachel yelled while holding her side unable to move. She knew she had to think quickly and do something before Black Ice killed her son. "I'll smoke that stuff. I'll do it!" she shouted.

"What?" Black Ice asked as he stopped burning Michael and turned to Rachel.

"I'll smoke crack with you just don't hurt my baby anymore," she pleaded.

Black Ice eyes opened wide while he looked at Rachel. He couldn't believe what he just heard. After months of beating his wife to get her to smoke crack, it took this to get her to change her mind. She wouldn't leave him. "If you're playing with me

Rachel I'll burn this little mother fucker so he wished he was dead." Black Ice said while shaking Michael's neck around like he was about to snap it.

"I'm not playing. I'll do it. Please just let our son go?" Rachel said with tears running down her beautiful brown face.

Black Ice smiled a devilish smile and knew in his heart she would do it. She'll be too scared that if she didn't that he would hurt the little punk. He dropped the hot comb on the floor and released his hand from Michael's neck. He looked at Rachel hold her side. He bent down and wrapped his arm around her and picked her up. He carried her to the bedroom. Michael screamed, "Mommy, don't smoke that stuff!" Those were the last words Rachel heard before Black Ice used the heel of his foot to kick the bedroom door shut. He put Rachel on their queen sized bed and walked over to the closet. He removed the floor board to his stash and pulled out two brand new glass pipes and a big piece of crack, the size of a baseball. He covered the stash back up and walked over to the dresser where a small glass mirror was. He carefully removed the crack from the glass jar and laid it on the mirror. He picked up a razor and started to cut small pieces of the crack. He stuffed the new pipes full of crack and walked over to Rachel. "Take it." Black Ice said handing her a glass pipe and a lighter. Rachel nervously brought the pipe up to her mouth and lit the end and inhaled.

"Don't play stupid with me. You've seen me do it enough times. Rachel smoked the crack still in pain and in tears.

Chapter 14

For many years, Rachel had to stay away from drugs. Her mother used dope. And when it got so bad for her, she left Rachel at Momma's house one day. Her mother never returned for Rachel and never saw her mother again after that day she left her. Black Ice watched her like a hawk. She could feel him watch her as she placed the pipe up to her mouth. Her hand shook as she held the lighter at the end and lit the pipe. Rachel took a tiny puff, inhaling the crack smoke.

"Rachel, don't fucking play with me. Hit that shit! You better take a big hit better than that, bitch!"

Rachel did as she was told. She sucked on the glass pipe as hard as she could. The crack smoke rushed down her throat and into her lungs. She began to cough from the hard hit. Black Ice smiled his infamous devilish smile as he watched her cough up smoke. Rachel felt lightheaded, but with an instant jolt of energy. Her eyes opened wide and the pain she felt earlier all over her body was gone. When Rachel looked up from coughing, Black ice looked in her eyes and saw the glassy look they had and he knew he had her. "Give me the pipe." He said as Rachel passed the pipe to him. She prayed that the worst was over. Black Ice repacked the pipe with more crack and passed it right back to Rachel. "Hit it again." He said. Rachel did what she was ordered to do. She hit the pipe again. They spent the whole night getting high together.

A month had passed; it amazed Black Ice how fast Rachel got hooked on crack. She was smoking more than he was now. Rachel smoked the entire crack up in the house. She couldn't fight the cravings. She needed to smoke every minute of the day. She lost a lot of weight. She went from 140 pounds to 90 pounds. She wore the same clothes every day. The tip of her fingers turned black from the heat of the glass pipe burning them. Her lips turned black too.

Michael watched as his beautiful mother started changing her looks from starting to smoke that funny smelling stuff. She looked like a stranger to him. She no longer made sure that he was fed or that he was wearing clean clothes. She didn't even pay him any attention anymore. Michael was forced to look after himself with his father running the stress and his mother locked in her bedroom getting high. She left him to take care of himself at the age of six. That made Michael's heart grow colder and hate his father even more. Michael lay on his pillow crying. He held in the tears. His stomach hurt and was in so much pain. There was no food in the house for him to eat. His mother only cared about smoking. She neglected to go shop for food. As Michael stomach growled, tears started flowing down his face and he prayed the hunger would go away once he fell asleep.

The next morning, Michael awoke to the smell of food. He opened his eyes and saw a bag on his dresser. He hopped out of his bed and ran to it. Inside there was a box with four chicken wings and fried rice from the Chinese restaurant. He knew his mother had gotten him the food. She'd be the only one to think about him once in a while. Times like that, reminded him of why he still loved his mother so much even though she hasn't been the same since she started smoking with his father. He quickly started eating his food to stop the hunger pains from his stomach making sure he didn't miss a crumb. He ate so fast that he bit his fingers twice while eating the chicken and rice. He smiled and rubbed his little belly. He wondered what his mother was doing. He wanted to go thank her for the food she left him. But, he thought she was probably smoking that stuff again.

Michael got up and walked to his mother's bedroom. When he heard screams, he listened carefully. It was his mother. He ran to the door of her bedroom and opened it. When he saw what she was hollering about, he knew she didn't need his protection. His mother's legs were up in the air resting on his father's shoulders as his father humped and pounded away on his mother. Michael had seen this enough times before to know that his mother was in no danger. He closed their bedroom door and walked into the living room. He covered his ears to diminish the sounds that were coming from his parents' bedroom.

After a half an hour, he blocked out the sounds all together. He sat on the couch staring at nothing. He thought to himself that when he gets older he would show his father while looking at the burn on his arm. It had bubbled up and dead skin was already starting to peel off causing itching and pain with the air on his skin. Michael swore he would kill him one day.

Just then, Black Ice came out of the

bedroom fully dressed. He walked into the living room and saw his son sitting on the couch just staring at the wall. A chill went down his back as he made his way to the door and left the apartment. Black Ice thought to himself that there was something wrong with that little mother fucker. He ain't right. Shit wasn't normal for a child to just be staring at walls. He knew in his heart that one day he would have to kill his son or his son would kill him.

Once outside of the apartment, Black Ice walked down the block and walked passed his white Lexus and turned the corner. He walked half way down the block and stopped in front of a brown Ford Taurus. He took some keys out of his pocket and opened the driver side door and hopped in the car. He was going to check on the block and see how these fools are running his shit. He owned the Ford Taurus, but no one knew he had it. It had tinted windows and it was easy for him to creep around without anybody knowing it was him. He started the car and headed to Mother Gaston Avenue.

He reached the block and slowed down and crept by slow. So he could notice everything that was taking place on the block. He smiled when he saw the young workers selling to the crack heads. He saw Ace standing by the project buildings watching every move that the workers were making. So, where's Caesar? He thought to himself. He always sees Ace on the block, but Caesar is nowhere to be found. He pulled off down the neighborhood. He cleared his mind. Everything was in order. The block looks good. Rachel is hooked on crack and that means she'll depend on him for the rest of her life. The only thing that he needed to do something about was that boy of his.

Black Ice drove around in deep thought and hoped to see Roxy walking down one of these streets. He will beat her ass and snatch her ass up once he finds her. In fact, he would kill that bitch. In deep thought, he noticed something out of the corner of his eye. He was driving too fast to get a good look. So, he circled the block. He knew that the car he saw was Caesar's. It was the only gold Acura Legend in the hood and no one else would be able to afford that car. When he rolled past the car again, it was his car. "What the fuck is Caesar doing over here?" he said aloud. He pulled up a long side of his car. His car was right outside of Ace's apartment building.

Why the hell would Caesar's care be parked outside of Ace's building? Black Ice wondered to himself with more questions to follow. He pulled forward and found a parking space ahead to keep in view of Caesar's car and Ace's apartment building. His mind was just racing with questions and not answers that he decided to sit up in his car and wait to see what was up with this scene. He pulled out a pack of Newport cigarettes. He took a cigarette out of the box and pulled out a jar of crack and stuffed some in the cigarette. After making sure the crack was nicely packed in, he lit it and inhaled. Taking in the entire smoke deep into his lungs he exhaled. The crack rushed into his system making his eyes open wide and got him nice and high. He kept his eyes on the apartment building and Caesar's car.

He watched a caramel woman walk up to the building and pressed the bell to be buzzed in. Black Ice sat up in his car seat to get a better look at the woman. He knew she couldn't see him because of the tint on his car windows. He knew the woman. It was Shelly. He knew that fat ass anywhere. Shelly was a hood rat and a gold digger. Black Ice had fucked her a few times and kicked her to the side. She'd do anything to

make a quick buck. Black Ice mind began
to race with thoughts. If Shelly was over
here, that meant that she's about to watch
Ace's kids. Shelly only came over to Ace
and Lisa's place to make some money by
babysitting while they went out. Black Ice
took another hit of his crack laced cigarette.
He watched Shelly get buzzed into the
building. He started rubbing his eyes and
rolled down the car window to let some of
the smoke out. Ever since he started
smoking this shit, he's gotten so paranoid he
thought to himself. He started to pull off
after bugging, but saw Caesar step out of the
building with Ace's youngest son in his arms
with Lisa following close behind. What the
fuck is going on here? Black Ice wondered.
Lisa, Caesar, and the little boy got into the
car and pulled away. Black Ice decided to
follow them making sure to stay two cars
behind them. If Mark, Ace's youngest son
in the car, was with them that meant Shelly
is only watching Aaron, the other son. He
kept following them until they reached King
Pizza Mall. He watched as Caesar got Mark
out of the car and grabbed Lisa's hand and
started walking towards the mall. Black Ice
parked his car and got out and followed
them making sure not to be seen. He made

sure to stay behind a few people who were shopping. He watched them enter the movie theater. They'd be there for a while he thought. Black Ice walked back out to the parking lot. He hopped in his car and pulled his glass pipe out and stuffed it full of crack and got high while waiting for them to come back outside.

Three hours later, he saw them come back out to the parking lot. Caesar's hands were full of shopping bags. They put everything into Caesar's car and drove off. Black Ice carefully followed them making sure not to be seen. Caesar stopped in front of Ace and Lisa's building again. Black Ice parked down the block and watched Lisa get out of the car with her son and went inside. A few minutes later, Lisa came back outside and got right back in the car and they left. Black Ice followed them to Pennsylvania Avenue to a hotel and parked. They got a hotel room. Black Ice knew that bitch was a slut. Once he was sure they were in their room, he hopped out of his car and walked over to Caesar's car. He pulled out a four inch pocket knife he carried that he got from Rachel's cousin, Brian that he killed and kept for himself. Black Ice stabbed both of the back tires of Caesar's car. He had to buy time for his next move and that would definitely keep them busy after their done fucking he thought to himself. He got back into his car laughing his evil laugh as he made his way back to Ace and Lisa's building.

Chapter 15

Once he got back to Ace and Lisa's apartment building, he parked the car down the block. He walked up to the building and rang the bell.

"Who's there?" Shelly asked through the intercom.

"Shelly, it's me Black Ice open up." He answered.

Shelly was quick to buzz him in thinking about the money she could make. Black Ice walked into the apartment since Shelly was waiting at the door with it wide open. "Hi daddy, what are you doing here?" she asked.

"I came to see you." He lied to answer her.

"It's been awhile since you fucked with me, ever since you started fucking with Roxy." She said.

"I didn't come here to listen to your comments. You know why I came here. Now, are you down or what?" Black Ice said.

"Yes, I'm down daddy." Shelly said moving to the side to let him in.

Black Ice couldn't help to look at Shelly's ass through her jeans as he passed her. She had a banging body, but she had a butt ass looking face. Everything looked good on her body, but her face. That was one of the reasons Black Ice quit fucking around with her.

"How did you get that scar on your face, daddy?" she asked as Black Ice covered his cheek with his hands.

"Don't worry about that," he replied.

"Where's Ace and the kids?" he asked.

"The kids are in their bedrooms asleep. So that would give us more than enough time to do us." Shelly said while licking her lips. Black Ice pulled out a cigarette and lit it while inhaling slowly.

"Can I get a cigarette, daddy?" she asked.

Black Ice handed her a cigarette and she lit it off his and inhaled. "This cigarette tastes funny." Shelly said while exhaling the smoke.

"But, that doesn't stop you from smoking it." Black Ice said with a smile on his face while he watched her smoke the cigarette laced with crack. All of his cigarettes were packed full of crack. He didn't hesitate to give Shelly one when she asked for a cigarette. It was something about turning a woman out on crack that made his dick hard. Shelly felt light headed and horny.

"Baby, you got another cigarette? That shit was good it got me high." Shelly said. Black Ice handed her another cigarette and watched her smoke it while he smoked too. When she was done smoking, he knew it was time to put his plan to work. There was no telling how long Lisa and Caesar would be at the hotel, but he flattened the tires on his car.

Shelly was sitting on the couch with that horny look in her eyes. She started to remove her clothes. Her shirt was the first to come off. Her tits popped out to show that she wasn't wearing a bra. Then her tight jeans came off and she wasn't wearing any panties either. Black Ice grabbed her by the neck and squeezed, choking Shelly. He pulled out a 9mm berretta and put the barrel to her face. "Open your fucking mouth." He said to Shelly. She gasped for air and didn't know what to do. Her head was spinning from the two cigarettes she smoked. She wasn't any fool thought. She knew Black Ice got down and would not test him. She slowly opened her mouth. Black Ice placed the barrel of the gun into it. "Now, suck it."

He said. Shelly started sucking the barrel of the 9mm gun like it was a dick. She hoped that he wouldn't pull the trigger. Black Ice watched Shelly work on the barrel of the gun, only turning him on even more.

While Shelly was sucking on the gun, Black Ice said, "Shelly, I know that Caesar is fucking Lisa. Don't try to even lie to me. What I don't know is for how long and what is the deal with Caesar and Mark. I want you to tell me everything I need to know. If I feel for one second that you're lying to me, I'm going to blow off your head. Are we clear?" he said to Shelly.

Shelly shook her head up and down as tears started rolling down her face. Black Ice smiled and put his hand around her neck and took the gun out of her mouth. Shelly wiped her eyes with the back of her hands. "Lisa's been fucking Caesar for three years now. I come over and watch the kids when she sneaks off with him."

"So, what's the deal with Mark? Why would they take Mark out today and leave Aaron here with you?" Black Ice asked.

"Because Mark is Caesar's son, not Ace's." she sniffled.

"What? Ace's youngest son, Mark, is not his? He's Caesar's son?" he asked.

105

"Lisa lied to Ace so he would continue to take care of her. So, now she gets money from Ace and Caesar." Shelly answered.

Black Ice started laughing and took out the glass pipe from his pocket. He stuffed the pipe with crack and passed it to Shelly. She took it and lit it and inhaled. Black Ice still pointed the gun at her. "But, I don't smoke crack." She said with tears running down her face.

"You do now. What do you think was in those cigarettes?" Black Ice laughed. "Smoke it, bitch!"

Shelly did what she was ordered to do afraid that he may still pull the trigger of the gun that was pointing at her. They continued to smoke the crack pipe. He led her to Ace and Lisa's bedroom and he got undressed. "Go ahead, do your thing, Shelly" he said.

Shelly grabbed his dick and started to suck it. The crack had her so high she almost forgot a few seconds ago Black Ice had a gun in her mouth. She deep throated his dick. "Mmm yeah" Black Ice moaned while grabbing the back of her head and pumping his dick with her mouth with her hair tangled between his fingers. "Suck that dick, bitch." He pumped even harder and she sucked even harder. Black Ice couldn't hold it anymore. He released his nut all in her mouth. Shelly just kept sucking and swallowing his cum. Black Ice got weak in the knees. "Damn girl, I forgot how good your head was. Turn around and bend over." Black Ice spit on his dick making it wet and slowly eased it inside her ass. Shelly moaned as he entered her and began to pump hard and fast. The crack had his dick hard as a rock again. Shelly put her face in the pillow and with both of her hands spread her butt cheeks. "Yes Daddy, fuck me. Fuck me." That only turned Black Ice on even more. He pounded harder and harder watched his dick disappear in her ass. "Yes, give me that ass you slut." He groaned. He grabbed her waist tight and pumped with all the strength he had. He quickly pulled out and grabbed his dick and stroked it to cum all over her ass. Shelly wiggled her butt cheeks like the slut she was. Shelly watched as Black Ice put on his clothes. He wanted to get out of the apartment before Lisa and Caesar returned. He got what he came for. He reached into his jeans pocket and threw some money and a few jars of crack with a pipe on the bed for payment to Shelly.

"Here take that. I know you're going to need it. You won't be able to fight the cravings." He said with an evil laugh and walked out of the bedroom.

He left the apartment building and hopped into his Ford Taurus. He took off thinking how he was going to use the information that he just learned about.

Shelly lay on the bed naked. She smelled the stench of sex and ass. Shelly looked at the end of the bed at the money. Her eyes moved to the jars of the crack. Her eyes were just stuck there. Her body began to shake and feel weird. It was like the crack was calling her. She tried to look away, but couldn't. She couldn't fight the craving. She picked up the pipe and stuffed it with crack and started smoking. She couldn't believe she was doing this shit she thought to herself. But, she kept smoking and inhaling until she was high again. She felt again her head being lightheaded and the craving died for a while. Ten minutes later, the craving was back and she started smoking again.

"Aunt Shelly, what are you doing?" a young voice said. Shelly jumped up with shock as she put the crack pipe behind her back and turned to see Aaron standing there.

She got so high that she forgot that she was still at Ace and Lisa's apartment to watch Aaron and Mark. "Why don't you have your clothes on, Aunt Shelly?" he asked. Shelly looked down and realized she was still naked.

"I was just in the shower. Go back in your bedroom and I'll be there in a minute." She said to him. Aaron did what he was told to do. Shelly got dressed quickly and put the money and the jars of crack in her purse. She found some incense and lit them in hopes that would kill the smell of crack smoke and sex before Lisa or Ace got home. Even with the shock of Aaron coming into the bedroom, her body quickly went into craving the crack again.

At ten o'clock in the evening, Ace walked into the apartment hoping to get a warm meal and a good fuck from his wife. "Lisa, why didn't you cook?" he asked as he headed to the bedroom. He opened the door to see Lisa wasn't there. He walked to the kid's bedroom and looked at his sons that were asleep. "Damn, where is this woman?" he said aloud. He heard a noise in the hallway bathroom. He went to the door and pushed it open. "Lisa, why didn't' you cook?" he started to ask. But before he got all the words out he stopped short as he watched Shelly inhaling smoke from a glass pipe. "Bitch, what the fuck are you doing?" he yelled.

Shelly tried to hurry and hide the pipe. "Yo, Shelly I know you're not smoking that shit now. And I damn sure know you're not smoking around my kids."

"No, and you mean kid!" Shelly snapped back at Ace while slipping with the words that just came out of her mouth.

"What you mean by saying just kid? Both of those boys are mine in that room."

Shelly realized what she said and went on to fix it. "Oh I'm just a little high. I've been smoking weed."

"That doesn't look like any weed to me and pretty sure I know what it is."

"Listen, I don't have time for this shit." Shelly said while grabbing her purse and walked out of the bathroom. She walked down the hall to leave the apartment. "Since you're here now, you can watch your kids. I'm tired of waiting for Lisa's ass."

"Yo, hold up. Where is Lisa? And how long has she been gone?" Ace asked with anger in his voice. He was mad that Lisa didn't tell him that she was going out today.

"Listen, all I know is she went out and paid me to watch the kids. As a matter of fact, she still owes me some money." Shelly said lying through her teeth. Lisa paid her earlier in the day. "So, are you going to pay me?" she asked while her hands went to her hips and her neck was rolling back and forth.

Ace dug into his jean pockets and handed her two hundred dollars.

"Thank you, and tell Lisa to call me." Shelly said as she made her way out the door and left. With a purse full of money, she wanted only to do one thing with it. Stop the craving.

An hour later around eleven o'clock, Lisa walked into the apartment hoping Ace hadn't made it home yet. "Shelly, I'm back."

"Yeah, back from where?" Ace questioned her walking out to confront Lisa. Lisa thought to herself, damn this nigga is home and made her way to the bedroom.

"So, where the fuck were you Lisa? And why didn't you tell me you were going out today? You know I hate when you do that shit and you keep doing it."

"I was out with my girl Brooke just

111

chilling."

"This fucking late and you were just chilling?" Ace asked getting all up in her face.

Lisa had to think fast before this nigga flips out on her. She knew she had fucked up. She planned on being home sooner, but after Caesar and her got done fucking they were trying to leave in a hurry. However, they couldn't go anywhere realizing the tires were slashed on Caesar's back car. They had to call a tow truck and waited on a cab to take her home. "Baby, I was stressed out. You know we need more money. And I want a bigger place for us and the kids. So forgive me, but sometimes I need to get up out of this house for a minute."

Ace felt guilty because he wanted to give Lisa the world and didn't have the money he needed to give her the dream house she wanted and more. Lisa saw Ace softening up. She knew the game she was playing on him was working and just needed to seal the deal. She began to remove her clothes and started rubbing on her tits. She started moaning and with a seductive voice said, "When was the last time you ate my pussy baby?" She lay down on the bed with her naked body and spread her legs wide open. Ace looked at Lisa's beautiful body and couldn't control himself. He came to her on the bed and slowly kissed her between her thick thighs. Lisa let out a soft moan as Ace made his way to her clit. Ace licked up and down teasing her body and felt Lisa quiver from the pleasure he was giving her. He slowly placed his lips around her clit and sucked on it. "Oh baby! Yes baby yes!" Damn this nigga could eat some pussy Lisa thought as she fell into ecstasy. Ace took her legs and pushed them up in the air so he could really eat her pussy out. He licked up and down around her clit and pussy. While using his tongue on her pussy, he took his fingers and spread her pussy lips apart so he could put his tongue deep inside her. Lisa moaned thinking of what she was just doing a few hours ago with Caesar. She still had Caesar's cum inside her dripping out of her pussy. And here she was with her man and he's eating her pussy and that nigga's cum. Damn she thought she was trifling letting this happen, but fuck it this shit was feeling so damn good. She grabbed the back of Ace's head forcing his tongue deeper inside her and had enjoyed every minute of it.

Chapter 16

Michael went to his mother's room and heard on the other side of the door her coughing. He knew she was alone because his father just came home to grab something and left again. Michael placed his little hand on the door knob and twisted. He pushed the door open. As soon as he opened the door, he was rushed by a cloud of thick, white smoke. He grabbed his head from the dizziness he was feeling from inhaling all the smoke. He coughed and said, "Mommy, mommy is you okay?" He walked towards his mother waving his hand to fan the some away from his face. He reached the bed where his mother was sitting and sucking on a glass pile.

Rachel didn't even notice her son standing close by. She was too busy smoking. Rachel thought she was tripping when she thought she heard a tiny voice call her mommy. She had been hearing voices and reliving the rape she went through.

Michael slowly touched his mother on her arm. "No Brian. Don't touch me! No!" Rachel used full force and kicked at Michael in the stomach sending him flying back onto the floor. "Aw, mommy it's me." He hollered in pain as tears ran down his face and held his stomach. Rachel snapped out of her daze when she heard her son crying. She put down the crack pipe and jumped out of bed and rushed to his side. "Baby, I'm sorry." She said to Michael to console him.

"Mommy, I just wanted to make sure you were okay." Michael said crying.

"I'm so sorry baby. Come with me. There's some food in the refrigerator that I'll heat up for you." Rachel said knowing that her son was hungry.

They walked into the kitchen and Michael sat down at the kitchen table. While his mother heated up his food on the stove. Rachel placed the food in front of him. She watched him eat. She felt so guilty. How did she let things get so bad? That she couldn't even feed her own son and she couldn't remember the last time she saw him in some new clothes. Rachel thought that she just hurt her son by kicking him in the stomach not even realizing he was in the room and hallucinating that it was her Uncle Brian trying to rape her again. And she can't stop the cravings of smoking crack. It calls her to get high and she can't fight it. Tears started rolling down her face and Michael looked up from his plate to see that

115

she was crying. "Don't cry mommy. Everything will be okay." Michael said.

Rachel knew she couldn't keep her son around this anymore. She ran back into his bedroom and packed a big bag full his clothes. She went back into the kitchen and grabbed Michael's hands. "Come on." She said.

"Where are we going mommy?"

"Baby, don't worry, just come on." Rachel and Michael walked out of the apartment. They walked four blocks down and made a left. Michael was surprised. He couldn't remember the last time he came outside of the apartment, let alone with his mother. His father didn't allow them to leave the apartment. And Michael wasn't even allowed to go to school. He learned how to read and write from his mother.

Rachel pushed the doors open and entered the Broadway Junction Train Station. Rachel put her hands inside her jeans pocket and realized she didn't bring any money to buy a train ticket. So, she jumped over the turnstile and Michael crawled under it. They began to walk, but out of nowhere a tall white police officer in a blue uniform stepped out in front of Rachel and Michael. "And where do you think you're going Miss?" he asked. Rachel stopped dead in her tracks. "Turn around and put your hands behind your back." The police officer ordered.

"What for?" Rachel asked.

"For not paying your fare and if you don't have the money to I'm going to take you to jail." He knew by the look on her face she was a crack head and didn't have the money to pay for her fare. So he would be taking her in. Rachel started to cry and said, "Listen, please don't take me to jail. I'm just trying to get my son to my grandmother's house for some food and clean clothes." The officer looked down at Michael for the first time and felt bad for the boy. He didn't know how these people could fuck up their lives by smoking crack. The kids are the ones that end up paying for their actions, the police officer thought to his self.

Michael saw his mother crying. "Don't take my mommy to jail. Take my daddy. He's the one that did this to her." Michael said while starting to cry for his mother. Rachel saw the officer's eyes never leave Michael as if he was in deep thought. She reacted to his stare quickly. "Look you see what he has on?" Michael had on some

117

old filthy jeans and a white t-shirt that he has been wearing for the last two weeks. Rachel turned her son around so his back was facing the officer. She pulled up his X-men briefs underwear and said, "You see? You see?" Rachel pointed the office to look down at Michael's underwear to see shit stain's spread all across the back of the boy's underwear. "And you want to take me to jail. I just want to help my baby."

The officer was feeling bad for Michael, but now his heart really went out to him. "Okay Miss. You can go. Just please take care of your son or just take him to your grandmother's house so he can get the help he needs."

"Thank you," Rachel said. She took Michael by the hand and started walking to the train. The officer watched as they disappeared. He felt so bad for the little boy. Rachel and Michael rode on the J-Train and switched over to the 3-Train. When the train stopped at Saratoga Avenue, they got off and walked five blocks down and stopped in front of an old beat up house.

They walked up to the door and knocked. After a few minutes, a small boy opened the door. He looked to be about the same age as Michael. "Hi, move Pooky."

118

Rachel said and made her way into the house with Michael following closely behind her. Rachel walked through the house and saw kids of all ages as she made her way to the big bedroom. She opened the door to the bedroom and looked at the old lady sitting in a chair watching Wheel of Fortune on the TV. "Momma" Rachel said. Momma looked at Rachel and then at Michael and said, "So, child you finally came back. They always come back." Momma sarcastically said.

It's been years since Rachel stepped foot in this house after Brian raped her and Black Ice killed him. She never returned after that. She kept in contact with her cousin Janet and that's how she knew who lived in Momma's house. However, she hasn't talked to Janet since she started smoking crack and lost contact. "Momma, where is Janet? I want to leave Michael with her." Michael looked up at his mother. She never left him with anyone before. She left him in the house by himself while she ran the streets at night to buy new crack pipes, but never just left him like she was going to.

"Child, Janet moved a while ago, but here." Momma said as she opened her purse and took out a piece of paper. "This is her number. She told me to give it to you, if you ever stopped by. She knew I wasn't going to call you. You look just like your mother did when she dropped you off here with me." Momma said and laughed. "So, what do you want?" Momma asked already knowing the answer.

"Momma, I need to leave Michael with you for a while. I can't take care of him right now." Rachel said.

"It's fine with me. It's just more money in my pocket book when I file for him for food stamps." Momma said in her proud voice.

"No mommy. I don't want to stay here. I don't know them." Michael said and busted out in tears. "I love you mommy. I won't come in your room anymore when you are smoking. I promise. Please mommy." Michael pleaded as he used his little hands to wipe the tears away.

"Listen baby. It will only be for a little while. I'll be right back to get you." Rachel said.

"But mommy" Michael pleaded.

"I got to go" Rachel said and started to walk out of the bedroom door. She headed down the hall to the front door. "I love you mommy." Michael's little voice grew fainter as she walked out of the house.

Rachel began to cry. She just did the same thing that her mother did to her. She began to run down the block and saw an alleyway, the same alleyway that Black Ice killed her Uncle Brian in many years ago. She walked in the alleyway and cried very hard and pulled out the glass pipe from her bra and stuffed it with crack. She lit the end and inhaled. The smoke rushed in her lungs and instantly relaxed her. For a few seconds, she forgot about her problems and pain. Ten minutes later, she remembered her problems and pain and she started sucking on the glass pipe again.

Chapter 17

"Oh, tomorrow it's on. So be ready J-Rock." Caesar said.

"I'll be ready son." J-Rock said.

"I'll holla at you tomorrow." Caesar said as he hung up the phone.

It's been three months since Caesar and J-Rock talked about killing Black Ice. Caesar looked at Ace and said, "He's at his weakest. It's now or never."

"You're right. I hope J-Rock knows what he's doing." Ace replied.

"Please nigga. Black Ice is cracked out. That nigga is a straight crack head. He shouldn't be getting money and no one should fear his ass no more. You see how he looks just like one of the fucking crack heads that our workers sell to."

"Yea, but he is still Black Ice." Ace stated. Ace knew all the shit that Caesar was talking about was true. He knew that Caesar was just as scared of Black Ice like he was or anyone else in the hood was for that matter. That's why he didn't try to kill Black Ice himself. Ace was starting to feel the real reason Caesar hated Black Ice. It was because Black Ice started fucking Roxy and he couldn't get no time with her.

Caesar and Ace sat in silence counting the money they made for the week in an apartment in Brownsville projects. Both of them were in deep thoughts. Ace was thinking about what he will do with all the money he'll be making and what kind of a house he'll be buying for Lisa and the kids. Caesar was thinking about how he came in Lisa's mouth earlier that day and how Ace would be kissing her later and he smiled.

"Yo, what are you smiling about son?" Ace asked.

"Nothing, my man, nothing" Caesar replied in a smooth tone.

Black Ice inhaled deeply and let the cigarette full of crack relax him. He stood in the lobby of building 234 in Brownsville projects with a brown paper bag full of money that he just collected from Ace and Caesar for the week. He was stuck in thoughts of how crazy of a week it had been. Rachel was smoking more crack than humanly possible as she was smoking an ounce of crack a day. Shit he didn't have in mind that when he made her start smoking it would be like that. She wasn't supposed to get this bad. Then the bitch took his son to Momma's house. He was going to go get him back he thought even as much as he hated the evil look his son has been giving him and for trying to kill him. He still loved Michael. The blood that was running thru his veins was his very own. Black Ice took the last of the cigarette and held the smoke in. He tossed the bud on the floor and pushed the building door open and walked outside. Once he was outside, he exhaled the smoke that was in his lungs and watched the smoke float in the air. He started walking through the projects to make his way out. He walked past a bench with three young thugs sitting on it. He took a quick glance at them as he passed them and got a feeling that something was wrong. He realized he didn't recognize any of those thugs on the bench. That was impossible he knew all the workers that worked for Caesar and Ace under him. "Shit it's the crack. It has me tripping. I'm paranoid as a mother fucker." He said to himself. His stomach started bubbling some more and he stopped in his tracks. "Fuck that I've lived this long because I listen to my gut." He said while turning around to walk toward the three thugs on the bench. He pulled out a cigarette on his way there. "Yo does one of you have a light?" Black Ice asked when he was face to face with them.

"Yeah" The tall men of the group said.

As Black Ice looked in the men's faces, an alarm went off in his head. He has seen these niggas from Picking Avenue. What the fuck were they doing over here? These niggas knew better than to try to get money over here. Right then and there Black Ice knew something was wrong.

One of the men held a lighter in his hand and flicked it as Black Ice bent over to light the cigarette. He could see from the corner of his eye one of the other men slowly reaching his hand to his waist. In the blink of an eye, Black Ice, let go of the bag of money he was carrying and pulled out his gun's, one in each hand, before the bag of money hit the ground. He squeezed the triggers of both guns at the same time, repeatedly. Bullets ripped through the men at the same time. Blood and pieces of skull covered his face and clothes as the bullets ripped through the faces of the men in front of him. Two bullets caught the man on the left of him in the neck and one in the heart making him slump over dead. The man behind the bench tried to react and reach for his gun, but was way too slow. Black Ice closed his arms together and had both guns aiming at him. The young thug found himself staring down the barrel of a 44 bulldog revolver and a nickel plated 9mm. "What the fuck are y'all niggas trying to do? Rob me? Y'all must be crazy!" Black Ice laughed.

"Yo man, it's nothing like that. J-Rock sent us to get at..." the young thug started to say. Black Ice ended those words by pulling the triggers on both guns. He turned around while keeping his guns aimed at the young thug and couldn't believe what he saw. Five men were running towards him shooting. Black Ice took a giant step onto the bench and leaped over it. He grabbed the young thug that was in front of him and put him in a one arm head lock. He started shooting back while using the body of the thug as a shield as rapid fire was coming at Black Ice left and right.

J-Rock let four quick shots from his gun hoping that they would find their mark. But every shot went into the thug that Black Ice was using as a shield squirming in pain as every bullet that was meant for Black Ice ripped through his body. He tried to get free of Black Ice's grip, but it was no use he was too strong. He let out a scream when the

126

last bullet ripped through him and his body went limp.

Black Ice felt the body get heavy and knew he was dead. He released his grip and raised his arms. Gunshots were flying all over from the oncoming gunmen squeezing their triggers. Bullets were flying all over the place as black Ice exchanged fire five bullets made their way to one of J-Rock's gunmen filling him up with lead and leaving him dead. J-Rock and Smoke saw their henchman go down so they took cover and let their two other gunmen attempt to approach Black Ice while he was firing his guns crazy.

A cop car road by the block and the cop looked in the projects to see the gunfight and reached for his radio and said, "Officer needs back up. Shot being fired in the projects." In no time, another cop car pulled up to the scene. The cops got out of their cars and the four of them made their way over to the gunfight with their weapons drawn and fired.

J-Rock watched as the back of one of his gunmen's head blew open leaving a whole the size of a baseball. He felt bullets whistle past his head. He looked back and saw the four white cops shooting at him and his men's direction. He ran behind a tree for cover. "Smoke, Smoke!" J-Rock yelled. Smoke lay's in the grass trying to get a good aim on Black Ice, but couldn't because he was using the bench for cover. "Yo, Smoke!" J-Rock yelled again.

Smoke looked over to see J-Rock calling for him and then saw the cops running towards them shooting.

"Grab the bag with the money and be out. Tell Juice to go after Black Ice." J-Rock yelled once he got Smoke's attention.

Juice was J-Rocks last gunmen and he was ducking in a bush reloading his gun. "Yo, Juice, you heard him." Smoke yelled at Juice.

Black Ice saw the four cops come and he was thankful because he was out of bullets. He used this opportunity and took off running.

"Follow him, Juice. Don't let him get away." Smoke said as Juice took off running after Black Ice. Smoke got up and ran for the brown bag. A bullet hit him in the leg. He grabbed the back of his leg and fired back at the cops making them duck and roll for cover. Smoke picked up the bag and ran to the nearest building. He ran through the lobby and knocked on a door inside. An old lady opened the door and Smoke shoved his way in. "Don't say shit and I won't shoot you grandma" Smoke said to the lady while pointing his gun at her and locking the door behind him.

J-Rock took off running across the street. "They're running." One of the cops said to the others. "I'll follow the one going across the street. You guys go after the others."

Juice ran as fast as he could to catch Black Ice. He saw him turn the corner around the building. Black Ice leaned on the building and quickly reloaded his guns. Juice was so busy trying to catch Black Ice he forgot about the cops that were chasing after him. Juice turned the corner of the building and something told him to turn his head to the side. He looked and saw Black Ice leaning against the wall with the guns pointed at him. Black Ice fired and watched as the shots ripped through Juice's body from the back and came out the front of him. The bullets sprayed in his chest and tore through his insides. Black Ice watched his body fall to the ground.

"We got another one." One of the cops yelled as the three of them approached. "Wait he is still moving." One of the cops said when he looked down and fired three shots into Juice's body while he was on the ground dying. Something caught the attention to one of the cops. He looked up at the side of the building to see Black Ice standing there with the guns pointing in their direction. "Move!" the cop yelled to his partner while he dived for cover. The warning came too late. Black Ice sent rapid fire toward the cop's bodies. They twisted and jerked as the bullets ripped through their bodies and faces like paper. They fell over dead right on top of Juice's body. The young cop lifted his head and looked up to see that his partners were dead and saw Black Ice run into the building. He grabbed the radio on his shoulder and pressed the button and said, "Officers down. I repeat Officers down. I need an ambulance and back up in Brownsville Projects." He requested as tears ran down his face. He got up slowly to run after Black Ice who ran into the building.

Chapter 18

Black Ice ran up the stairs to the
second floor and laughed. A sense of
pleasure overwhelmed him when he saw the
cops fall over dead. He ran down the long
hallway to the back stairway and ran down
the stairs to the back exits of the building.
He could hear the sirens of more police cars
arriving around the building. He quickly
went to the next building and ran up to the
fourth floor and knocked on apartment 4C of
the building. The door opened, "Ray Ray
move let me in." Black Ice shoved his way
in the door. Ray Ray locked the door behind
him.

The young police officer lost Black
Ice at the first building on the second floor.
He didn't know where he went. He didn't
know the project buildings and the back
exits. He went outside and cried for his
partner's lives that were lost as he heard the
sirens coming closer for the backup he
needed, but it was too late. He already lost
Black Ice.

The S.W.A.T team and uniform cops
surrounded the Brownsville Projects.
Detective Roy was an overweight cop that
was in charge of the investigation. He

approached the young cop that chased Black Ice inside the building. "What's your name officer?" Detective Roy asked they young cop.

"Officer Reed sir" He answered.

"Okay Officer Reed, tell me what the fuck is going on? Why do we have three dead cops and six gunmen?" Detective Roy asked.

"Did you say three dead cops?" Officer Reed asked. He only knew of his partner and one other man.

"Yes there are three dead men of our own. Start from the beginning." Detective Roy ordered.

"My partner and I were driving by when we saw the gunfight going on. He jumped out of the car to try to get things under control."

"Do you know what the gunfight was about?" Detective Roy asked.

"No sir, but all the gunmen seemed to be shooting at one person. He was dark skin and really black. He had two guns and was shooting right back at all of them like crazy." Office Reed started.

Detective Roy's heart jumped a beat. He knew who ran this hood, Black Ice. He's wanted to take Black Ice down for years, but there were never any witnesses when a murder showed up and everybody knew Black Ice did it. But, no one was foolish enough to snitch on him. Detective Roy still remembered the pair of hands they found tied up on the power lines a few years back. "Okay officer, keep going. Tell me how the other two cops ended up dead."

"We all..." he began until interrupted by Detective Roy.

"What do you mean 'we all'?"

"Well sir the other two officers and myself started chasing the tall man that everybody was shooting at. The suspect we were chasing turned around and fired on us." He swallowed hard. He needed to give another reason why other than that they shot the young man on the ground that was still alive out of cold blood. He sure wasn't going to tell him that. He continued, "Once the suspect fired at us we exchanged gunfire and killed him. My partner walked up to him to disarm him. When I turned my head the other suspect that the man we killed was chasing, was leaning up against the building wall in a shadow with two guns pointed at us. I tried to warn the other officers, but it was too late. The suspect killed them in cold blood. I was on the floor and took cover and fired back at him. He, meaning Black Ice, ran into that building right there. I followed him inside, but lost him. He was laughing sir the whole time running."

"Officer Reed if you saw the suspect again, would you be able to point him out in a line up?" Detective Roy asked.

"Yes sir I would. He had the evilest eyes I've ever seen."

Detective Roy turned to the S.W.A.T team and ordered them to search the building. He ordered the uniform cops to go door to door ordering everybody out of their apartments and to search through the apartments. Detective Roy knew now for sure that the shooter of the death of the cops had to be Black Ice. The evil eyes and the laughter the officer talked about could only be one person. He thought I'm going to get that nigga one way or the other, if it's locking his ass up or putting his body in a body bag.

Chapter 19

Ray Ray was in the mix of the crowd
of noisy people around the crime scene.
After hearing everything he needed to get
the news to Black Ice. He slowly walked off
and headed back to his building. He ran up
the four flights of stairs into his apartment
on the fourth floor. He locked the door.
"Yo, it looks bad out there." He said as he
turned around to face Black Ice who was on
the couch smoking crack out of his pipe.
    "What the fuck you mean it looks
bad. I sent you out there to go details. Now
tell me what it looks fucking bad out there
means." Black Ice hollered.
    "Chill Black Ice" Ray Ray said in a
pleading tone. "The cops and the S.W.A.T
team are searching the building next to this
one. They are making everybody come out
of their apartments and they are looking for
you. They don't know you are over here."
    "What you mean they are looking for
me. Do they know it was me?" Black Ice
asked.
    "No, not really, but that fat fucking
Detective Roy is out there and you know he
has it hard up for you for years. And there's
this young white office named Reese, or

Reed. He told him he the guy who shot the cops and could point him out in a line up."

"Really?" Black Ice said while rubbing his chin. "Here take this." He threw a piece of crack the size of a small rock to Ray Ray. "Here this is what I need you to do. I can't leave yet and go outside. The projects will be crawling with police for a day or even more. What I want you to do is follow that young cop back to the precinct and then to his house and write the address down. I'll pay you good." Black Ice said.

"But, Black Ice how am I going to follow him I don't have a car." Ray Ray asked.

Black Ice pulled out a set of keys from his jeans pocket and handed them to Ray Ray. "Take these. There's a brown Ford Taurus with tinted windows parked on Shutter Avenue."

"I didn't know you had a Ford Taurus." Ray Ray said.

"Don't worry about that and get fucking moving! Go now!" Black Ice yelled at Ray Ray. With that Ray Ray was out of the apartment and headed down the block and around the corner to Black Ice's car.

Officer Reed went to the 77 precinct

and changed his clothes in the locker room. He felt as if all eyes were on him. His partner and another officer are dead. He felt like it was his fault. He quickly got dressed and put his uniform in his locker and exited the precinct. He walked out into the parking lot and walked up to his Toyota Camry. He pulled off thinking to himself "Damn, I can't believe this shit. I lost my partner." Tears started rolling out of his eyes making it hard for him to see where he was driving. "If I only would have warned him in time, Billy would still be alive." He said to himself. He stopped at a red light and closed his eyes. Black Ice's laugh echoed in his head. He could still see clearly Black Ice pointing the two guns at him and the other officers. "His eyes, those evil looking eyes, how could a man be so evil?" he said aloud. Then he flashed back about a month ago, when he was on duty at the Broadway Junction Train Station. He was getting ready to arrest a woman for hopping the turn style. The flashback went to the young little boy and his eyes. He remembered his eyes and thought they had the same look as the eyes he saw today. The boy's words echoed in his head. 'Don't arrest my mommy it was my daddy. Blame him. Get him.'

Officer Reed was so absorbed in his thoughts of losing his partner and remembering events up to this day that he about missed his turn into his neighborhood. He pulled up in his driveway of his house. He lived in an, all Jewish neighborhood and was very proud of it. There wasn't a black person around for miles the way Brooklyn used to be. He pondered what he was going to tell his wife as he got out of his car and walked up to the door.

He opened the door to his house. He never noticed the brown Ford Taurus that followed him and was parked across the street from his house. Ray Ray sat in the parked car and pulled out a pen and wrote down the address on a piece of paper. He put the paper in his jeans pocket and grabbed his crack pipe that was in the passenger seat next to him. He broke a piece of crack off the big rock Black Ice gave him and stuffed it in his pipe. He held the fire to the end and inhaled deeply and exhaled.

Chapter 20

J-Rock picked up the phone on the third ring. "Yo, who this?" he answered. "Yo, what the fuck happened today? I heard that nigga got away." The voice on the line yelled.

J-Rock now knew it was Caesar on the phone. "Yo, who the fuck are you barking on? Calm the fuck down, alright?" J-Rock said.

"Alright, I just want to know what went down today." Caesar replied.

"Yo, you said that nigga was slipping. That fool may be on crack, but he was on point. I had three of my men sitting on a bench waiting for him to come out of the building. We all were going to rush him at once from all sides, but somehow Black Ice knew something was wrong and started shooting my men that was sitting on the bench. That nigga even had two guns on him shooting all crazy. He even used one of my men as a shield." J-Rock started explaining.

"Yo, I heard that nigga killed three cops." Caesar said.

J-Rock went quiet for a minute because he knew that he killed one of the cops, but wasn't about to tell Caesar that. "Yea, yea that nigga was wild." J-Rock replied.

"Yo, I hear the cops are looking for him about those dead cops. So, this shit still might work out for us. We just have to lay low until they get him and all the heat dies off." Caesar said.

"I'm with that. I'll hit you up later." J-Rock said hanging up the phone.

J-Rock lay back on the bed and wondered where the fuck was Smoke with that bag of money. He didn't get caught today and he would have heard something by now. It's drawing near the day he takes over Brownville Projects and kills Caesar.

Chapter 21

Rachel was high pacing back and forth in her bedroom. It has been three days and she hasn't heard or seen a sign of Black Ice. Rachel walked back to the closet and removed the floor board. There were still two ounces of crack and a lot of money. She pulled the zip lock bags of crack out and covered the stash and sat back on the bed. She thought to herself two ounces of this shit isn't going to last. Where the fuck is Black Ice? She jumped off the bed when she heard a knock at the door. She walked to the door and looked through the peep hole. There stood a detective and four uniform cops with him.

Rachel slowly opened the door. "Yes, may I help you?"

Detective Roy looked down at the skinny Rachel with disgust. Damn crack head he thought to himself. "Yes, you can. Help us. We're looking for Michael David Ice, Sr., or Black Ice as you and everybody else refer to him as."

"Okay. So, what do want with him?" Rachel asked.

"Listen lady is he her or not?" Detective Roy said while trying to peek over her shoulder.

"No he is not here." Rachel said.

"Well, if you're lying and he's hiding here, you'll be arrested too when we get him. We have an eye witness saying he's behind the death of two officers."

"I don't know what you're talking about. And Black Ice doesn't live here." Rachel said and shut the door in Detective Roy's face.

"Bitch" Detective Roy said. "Come on let's go get a warrant and rush this place. I know that bitch is lying." Detective Roy said to his officers as they walked away from the door.

Rachel's mind was racing with all kind of thoughts. She knew that they'd be back. What to do? She quickly grabbed one of Black Ice's duffle bags and went to the stash in the closet and pulled all the money out and dumped it into the bag. Then she looked at the three guns in the stash and decided to take them and put them into the bag too. She went to the dresser and saw a drawer full of different kinds of keys, all shapes and sizes. Rachel knew Black Ice had apartments all over with money and to stash his inventory. She even heard from rumors that he had a house full of money and body parts that he collected off his victims. Rachel didn't know if it was true or not, but she wouldn't be surprised if it was true. However, she only knew of two of his apartments he had in someone else's name. She needed to make up her mind where she was going before the cops come back to rush this place.

Chapter 22

Black Ice woke up to the smell of
rotting flesh. The smell made his head spin.
He looked around to see that he was still at
Ray Ray's apartment. He looked at his hand
and clothes that were covered in blood. He
walked into the kitchen following the rotten
smell. He looked down on the kitchen floor
to see Ray Ray decomposing body with five
knives stuck deep into his back. Black Ice
looked at his body thinking someone was
trying to make his death into art work or
they were just having fun at killing him.
Little fat maggot's crawled around eating the
body. Black Ice stepped over the body and
turned on the water in the kitchen sink and
washed his hands and face. He remembered
Ray Ray coming home with that cop's
address and getting high with him. But,
doesn't remember killing the old mother
fucker and that had to have four or five days
ago that he remembers. He thought he must
have blacked out or something. The only
thing he knew he needed to do now was get
the hell out of that apartment before the
neighbors started to smell his body. He
grabbed his things and left the apartment
heading for one of his secret apartments to

pick up some things.

Officer Reed was driving home after a long day at work. He couldn't wait until Detective Roy would get the search warrant tomorrow. He was one of the officer's that was with Detective Roy that visited Rachel earlier today. He knew he saw that woman before. He watched the darkness cover the night sky as he pulled up in his driveway. He was hoping to come home to a nice hot cooked meal. He put his key in the door and opened it and stepped in. SMACK! Officer Reed slumped over as he felt the pain for the back of his head. SMACK! SMACK! Officer Reed hit the floor and tried to keep his eyes opened, but it his world went dark as he passed out from the blow to his head one final time. The sounds of crying could be heard by Officer Reed. He shook his head and opened his eyes. The house was dark and he clearly couldn't see what he was looking at. He tried to get up, but realized he was hog tied with duct tape. He heard the cries of a woman and looked across the living room floor. He could see a white ass up in the air and a man humping and pounding in and out of her. He heard the man say to the woman, "You like that don't you? Don't you?"

"Yes." The voice of the woman moaned.

"You have never felt a dick this big. Have you?" the man said.

"No." the lady let out a moan. The man pounded harder and harder and pulled out and busted his nut over her pussy. "I want more." She moaned.

"I'm sorry, my dear, but that's all you're getting. Now get the fuck up."

Officer Reed couldn't see them clearly, but the woman's voice he knew. The living room lights came on and Officer Reed couldn't believe his eyes. There was his wife sitting naked on a chair. Then he looked over to the man and it was the same man that killed his partner and the other cops a week ago.

"Oh I see your eyes are opened, Mr. Reed." Black Ice said while putting his clothes back on. He then turned to Mrs. Reed and duck taped her to a chair.

"What the fuck is going on?" Officer Reed yelled in anger knowing his wife just enjoyed being fucked by Black Ice.

Barbara, Officer Reed's wife, just sat there quiet with a shameful look on her face.

"First of all, I want you to stop fucking yelling. I'll go upstairs and get the

146

newborn son of yours. What is he eight months?" Black Ice said.

"No! Please don't hurt him." Barbara cried.

"Just shut the fuck up!" Black ice demanded. Barbara got quiet. "I see Officer Reed. You don't be fucking your wife right or you have a little dick." Black Ice laughed. "She loved every minute of me fucking her."

Officer Reed was burning up with anger, but didn't want to say anything out of fear of what this crazy man may hurt his son. Black Ice saw Officer Reed's face turn red and knew he was getting to him. So, he decided to rub it in some more.

"I've been fucking your wife for almost eight hours now waiting for you. When you came home, I hit you with my gun and was going to get straight to business that I came here for, but she kept begging and begging for more of this black dick." Black Ice said while grabbing his crotch.

Officer Reed looked up in his wife's face and could see what Black Ice said was all true. Barbara held her head down afraid to make eye contact with her husband.

Deep down inside she enjoyed every inch of that black dick she got today. But, she'll never say it. Her story will be that he raped her. Then she thought that he would fuck her one more time before he left as her pussy got wet just by the thought.

"So, you're going to point me out in a line up? Are you?" Black Ice laughed. Officer Reed remembered that laugh the day his partner was killed by this man. It kept echoing in his head ever since. Black Ice picked up the duct tape from the floor and taped Barbara's mouth. Her eyes grew wide open when she saw Black Ice pull out a six inch knife and come towards her. "I need something to remember you by my dear." Black Ice took hold of one of her breasts and licked the pink nipple until it was nice and hard. Barbara let out a soft moan of pleasure for the feeling of his tongue on her nipple. Then a sharp pain replaced the sweet pleasure she was feeling. She tried to move, but was duck taped to the chair. All she could do was squirm in place. She let out a scream, but it was muffled by the duct tape over her mouth. Black Ice sliced away at her nipple and pulled as hard as he could until he had her nipple in his hand. He put his tongue across the piece of flesh and the blood smeared all over his lips.

Barbara screamed and groaned as she rocked back and forth in the chair in extreme pain. Her blood dripped down her naked body from her missing nipple. Office Reed's eyes grew wide as he watched Black Ice remove his wife's nipple from her body. He tried to wiggle free from the duct tape, but it was tied up to tight.

Black Ice grabbed Barbara's ear. She tried to move her head, but it was locked in his grip. Her tears rand down her face from fear and in pain. Black Ice smiled and with one slice removed her ear from her head. She yelled as the blood poured out from the detachment on the side of her head. She felt as if she was going to pass out from the loss of blood and the pain.

Then crying was heard from the little baby upstairs. "It looks like someone woke the baby. He'll just have to join the party." Black Ice said.

"NO!" Officer Reed yelled as Black Ice made his way upstairs. A few minutes later, he returned with the baby curled up in his arm. "You have yourself a cute baby, Officer Reed." Black Ice made his way over to Barbara who was crying and trying to stay awake and not pass out. Black Ice looked into both Barbara and Officer Reed's eyes. He saw both pleading in their eyes both begging him not to hurt their baby. Black

Ice pulled out a Beretta 9mm with a silencer on it. He put the gun to the baby's head.

"NO! NO!" both screamed. An orange flash came out of the gun as a bullet tore through the baby's chest. Black Ice released the newborn baby and both Barbara and Officer Reed watched as the baby hit the floor. Officer Reed wiggled around on the floor full of rage. "Don't worry little pig. I'll make my way to you." Black Ice raised his gun to Barbara's forehead. She was crying looking at her baby on the floor. She never looked up at the gun. The bullet shredded through her skull and sent pieces of her brain flying everywhere.

Black Ice walked over to Officer Reed and bent down next to him. "You should have kept your mouth closed, pig. It's a shame I had to kill your wife. She had some good pussy and she could suck some dick." Black Ice laughed.

Officer Reed didn't hear a word Black Ice said. His mind and heart were lost in pain over the loss of his son and wife. Black Ice stood back up and aimed his gun at Officer Reed and let off five shots and two quick ones in rapid succession. He watched the bullets tear through his body and him jerk around until he died. Black Ice grabbed

Officer Reed's work bag and grabbed a few things in the house he needed. He picked up the chunks of flesh and put it in the bag and left the house with an evil grin on his face. He laughed and hopped into his Ford Taurus and pulled off.

Chapter 23

    "Yo, what the fuck are going to do? It's been three weeks now and the cops still haven't caught Black Ice. Caesar do you think he knows that we had something to do with that?" Ace asked nervously.

    "Naw, he doesn't know. If he did we'd be dead already." Caesar replied.

    "You heard the cops rushed his apartment and they still couldn't find him, even his son and that bitch are nowhere to be found. What are we going to do?" Ace continued while leaning back on the passenger seat of Caesar's car. He was more than nervous. He was scared shitless. He knows how Black Ice gets down and he damn sure didn't want to be one of his victims with a body part missing. Shit if it wasn't for Caesar and Lisa talking him into this shit, he wouldn't even have been down for it. Lisa always wants more and more money. Ace thought to himself.

    "Listen Ace, J-Rock is on the low now. And we can't get him to go try to kill Black Ice again, even if he did find him. Black Ice will be on point, but I got a plan." Caesar said.

    "What?" Ace replied.

"Black Ice hasn't been around to pick up this money from the spot in three weeks. This is what we do. We keep running the spots and collect all the money. He will pop up one day to get his money. You know Black Ice can't stay away from his money. Shit that nigga would kill us if he thought we didn't have his money, even if he is in hiding. So, when he comes for the money we will be waiting for him." Caesar said.

"What the fuck you mean? We will be waiting for him?" Ace asked.

"I mean we have to hill him ourselves." Caesar said.

"What?" Ace yelled. "Getting someone to kill his was one thing, but now you want us to hill him?"

Caesar got into Ace's face. "This shit is not a game nigga. If you want to make this fucking money to buy Lisa a house or anything else, we have to put in work. I want that spot for myself, and nothing is going to stop me. Are you in or what?" Caesar said while slowly reaching for his gun on his waist.

"Yea, man I'm in, but how did you know I want to buy Lisa a house. I don't remember telling you."

"Oh, you must have said something to

153

me. How else would I have known?"

"Yea, yea right" Ace replied, but knew he never said anything to Caesar about him wanting to buy a house. How the fuck he knows that, I only told Lisa he thought. As he got out of Caesar's car and headed towards his own car, "Remember be ready." Caesar hollered.

Chapter 24

Rachel's bottom lip trembled for the craving she was feeling. She already smoked the two ounces she had left the apartment with, but found one of Black Ices' stash spots in one of the apartments she went to. She smoked the entire crack in the stash spot, but there was money on top of money in that spot. She would take the money out of the stash for her house. She was going to buy crack off the street. Rachel sat on the bed and cried. She couldn't fight it and she wanted to. She cried out loud. She started thinking of her baby, Michael. She couldn't remember the last time she saw him. She missed him very much. Tears started flowing down her face. She held her hands to her face and cried. She had to figure out something. She had to.

She then thought that she needed to leave this apartment before Black Ice found her here. She had to get her baby back. She went through her bag and found a piece of paper with a number written on it. She picked up the house phone and dialed the number. "Hello." The voice said on the other end of the phone.

"Janet?" Rachel asked.

"Yes. Who is this?" Janet asked back.

"It's Rachel."

"Oh my God, Rachel I miss you. What took you so long to call?" Janet said.

"Janet, I......I need your help."

Janet could hear Rachel starting to cry. And knew it was serious. "What do you need? I'll do anything for you cousin."

"I need a place to stay and your help." Rachel started to say.

"Say no more. Where do you want me to come and pick you up?" Janet asked.

"Meet me at Momma's place." Rachel said and hung up the phone and grabbed the bag with money and headed out the door.

Michael cried for two weeks straight and every now and again when he went to bed. He thought of his mother. He'd use a dirty pillow that he laid on to wipe away the tears. She promised that she would come back to get me. It had been five weeks and his mother still hasn't come back to get him. Michael heart became even colder every day he went without his mother's love. He blamed his father for making her the way she was, but deep down he started to hate her as well for never coming back for him. He didn't care that she missed his birthday

156

and he didn't get a birthday cake or gift. All he wanted was his mother's love and to be taken away from Momma's house.

Michael hated Momma's house. He was forced to shit in a bucket and dump it outside in the back yard. Pooky, his cousin, and Michael had to share a bed. Pooky always pissed the bed. And Michael would wake up all wet and smelled like piss. When he told Momma, she just laughed at him and called him a child of a crack head. She say, "Boy don't you know that you're not going to be better than even the shit I push out because you are a child of a crack head." Those words broke Michael's heart at seven years old being told he wasn't going to be better than shit. He felt more pain then he should. So, he turned the pain into anger and unleashed it. He started kicking Pooky out of the bed. He wouldn't let his cousin sleep in the bed anymore. "Pooky, you can't sleep in this bed anymore. I'm tired of you pissing on me."

"You can't tell me what to do." He tried to climb back on the bed, but Michael curled his hands in a fist. And with all his might and strength hit Pooky like he saw his father do to his mother so many times. Pooky went flying backward after he struck him with his fist. He hit the floor hard leaving Pooky crying holding his eyes.

"I'm telling Momma." Pooky said crying.

"Go ahead. You still ain't sleeping in this bed."

Pooky got up and ran to Momma's room holding his eye. Michael followed behind him. Poky found momma in her room in her chair watching a talk show. "Momma, Momma. Michael kicked and punched me and said I couldn't sleep in the bed next to him no more."

"Boy, stop your fucking crying. You damn child of a crack head." Momma turned her head towards Michael. For some reason, she hated Michael, maybe because he was Rachel's baby or because he had Black ice blood running through him. She heard rumors that Black Ice killed her youngest son, Brian. She didn't know if it was true or not, but she still hated Black Ice just from the rumors.

Momma knew Brian was raping all the boys and girls in the house, but she didn't care. She didn't care because she thought that just because the kids were children of crack heads it didn't matter. "Listen you little mother fucker. You don't

158

tell anyone in this house what to do in this house. If anyone is going to sleep on the floor, it's going to be you!" Momma yelled while looking into Michael's eyes. Momma looked deep into them and saw no fear and someone that was cold hearted. Michael smiled a devilish grin. Momma swore she could see the devil look back at her. Her heart skipped a beat and started beating faster. She gasped for air while grabbing at her chest. "Pooky.....Pooky" She said out of breath. "Go grab my pump on the dresser."

Pooky began to walk to the dresser. He felt hands wrap around his neck and pull him back being shoved to the floor. Michael jumped on top of Pooky and began to hit him whit his fist again and again. When Michael got tired, he got off of him. Pooky lay on the floor crying in pain. "Now you stay there until I tell you to move and you are going to sleep on the floor, not me." Michael yelled.

Momma watched the boys while gasping for air as if she was going to pass out and die. She fell to the floor and tried to crawl over to the dresser herself. Michael slowly walked to the dresser and grabbed the pump and bent down next to Momma and put the pump in front of her face. Momma wheezing tried to reach for the pump. Michael pulled it back. "If you ever call my mother a crack head or talk to me wrong again, I will let you die."

"I....I won't." She wheezed. Michael handed her the pump. She placed it to her mouth and pressed down on the pump. She let the medicine fill her lungs and she repeated until she was breathing normal. Momma said, "You're just like your father." She got up and stepped back from Michael out of fear.

"Don't say that!" Michael yelled and walked out of the room and went to bed.

Chapter 25

Rachel walked through Momma's door early in the morning. She made her way past the dirty clothes and the garbage on the floor to the room where she knew Michael would be sleeping. She looked down on the floor and saw Pooky lying there sound asleep. She sat down on the bed next to her son watching him sleep. She had tears rolling down her face thinking how much she missed Michael. She rubbed his head.

Michael dreamt that he heard his mother's voice and tears rolled down his face while he was still asleep. He opened his eyes to wipe the tears, but he felt a soft hand wipe them for him. He sat up rubbing his eyes not believing what he was dreaming. But, it wasn't a dream. His mother was sitting right next to him. He jumped into her arms about knocking her off the bed. All the hate and pain he was feeling just went away feeling his mother embrace him in her arms. "Come on baby. We have to go." Rachel said to Michael.

"What about my clothes?" Michael asked.

"Leave them here. We're going to get

you some new ones." She answered.

Pooky woke up from the noise and watched Michael and Rachel leave from the bedroom. "I'll get you one day." Pooky grumbled to himself as he started to cry.

Momma watched Rachel and Michael leave her house and was more than happy to see Michael leave. "That child is pure evil." She thought to herself.

When they got outside, Rachel held Michael's hand and led him to a gray two door Nissan Pathfinder. He opened the door and crawled up in the SUV. Rachel reached for the seatbelt and buckled her son in. Michael looked at the driver. She was a pretty young woman. She almost looked just like his mother, until his father made her smoke that stuff. "Mommy, who is she? And where are we going?" Michael asked.

"This is my little cousin, baby. Her name is Janet." Rachel explained.

Janet heard her name and she looked back at Michael and smiled the most beautiful smile Michael has ever seen next to his mother's smile. "Hi Michael" Janet said.

"Hi." Michael said.

"We're going to a small town called Amityville in Long Island. That's where I

162

live and you are going to help me and your mommy, get herself better." Janet said to Michael.

"You mean you don't want to smoke that funny smelling stuff anymore, Mommy?" Michael asked.

"That's right." Rachel replied.

Michael looked at both woman and smiled real big. That made him so happy. He was willing to do anything to get things back to where they were before his mother started smoking that stuff.

Chapter 26

J-Rock was so scared that he never left his apartment since the attempted killing of Black Ice that was not successful. He still hadn't heard from Smoke. The word on the street was he dipped out after taking the bag of money that Black Ice dropped that day. It's been six weeks already and the cops still haven't caught Black Ice to bring him in for questioning. J-Rock knew he shouldn't have messed with Caesar and Ace's ass and crossed Black Ice. J-Rock needed some ass and wanted a quick fuck. So, he called Shelly. He heard that she started smoking crack and he fucked her a few times in the past. He knew all he had to do was give her a little bit of money, but now that he knew she smoked crack it would be even cheaper.

J-Rock heard the doorbell ring at his door. He got up and walked to the door and looked through the peek hole. There she was. Shelly lost weight, but her ass was still there he thought as his dick got hard just by the sight of her thick ass. He opened the door and Shelly stepped forward and fell right into J-Rock and knocked them on to the floor. J-Rock looked up not knowing what was going on. He got chill's running up and down his spine when he looked up to see Black Ice standing over them. "Get up Shelly!" Black Ice ordered her. Shelly nervously stood up leaving J-Rock on the floor. "Take this and be on your way." Black Ice told Shelly. He handed her a small zip lock bag full of crack with his devilish smile on his face. Shelly grabbed the bag and walked out the door. Black Ice slapped her on her ass while she walked by him. Then he closed the door and locked it while his gun was still pointing at J-Rock. "Get the fuck up!"

J-Rock did what he was told. "Walk to the bedroom. If you make any funny moves, I'll blow so many holes in your head. You'll have to have a closed coffin at your funeral." Black Ice ordered J-Rock.

Once in the bedroom, Black Ice made J-Rock lay on the bed. He took duck taped him to the bed wrapping his arms, chest and legs tight to the bed. "So you want to kill and rob me?" Black Ice yelled.

"No Black Ice. It wasn't me. It wasn't me." J-Rock begged him.

Black Ice hit him in the nose with the butt of the gun making it bleed instantly. He pulled out his six inch knife and grabbed J-Rock's cheeks so tight that he was forced to open his mouth. Black Ice put the knife in his mouth and started cutting the inside. J-Rock squirmed trying to get away from Black Ice's grip. His mouth was full of blood. Black Ice dropped the knife on the bed. He used his hand and grabbed J-Rock's tongue and pulled at it.

J-Rock's screams filled the apartment. He felt his tongue being ripped out of his mouth. J-Rock laid there crying and squirming around while blood was pouring out of his mouth. "See you thought you can taste the money on my block. Now you won't taste shit in your life now as a matter of fact!" Black Ice picked up the knife again. He grabbed J-Rock by the head and put the knife up to his eye. J-Rock squeezed his eyes shut. But, Black Ice used his thumb to open his eyelids. He stuck the knife in his eye. "Now, this will be the last thing you will ever see!"

Chapter 27

Michael watched both women walk down stairs to the basement with a duffle bag in each hand. Michael stood by the door on top of the stairs as his mother and her cousin hid the bags. "Damn, Rachel, these are heavy. How much money is in these bags?" Janet asked.

"Altogether there is about seventy thousand dollars, but there are some handguns in there too."

"You took the handguns too?" Janet asked with a concerned voice.

"You never know I may need them, but I doubt it." Rachel replied.

"Rachel you're going to get really mad and angry at me because I'm going to lock you in a room until I feel all the cravings are out of your system." Janet wanted to make Rachel understand what she needed to do to help her.

Rachel looked down at her feet. "Do what you need to do to help me. I need to get better for my son. He needs me and I know I need to change this from within myself."

"Rachel you can't blame yourself it was Black Ice who did this to you and together as a family we're going to make it pass." Janet assured Rachel.

The next few weeks were hell for Rachel. Her body was cleaning out her system. She screamed and yelled to come out so that she could go and find some crack to smoke. She pleased and cried, but Janet never opened the door. The only time she opened the door was to give Rachel her meals.

Michael's heart was breaking hearing his mother go through all the emotions. He wanted to help her, but didn't know how. He spent the day playing football in the backyard with Janet's boyfriend Jay Jay. Michael hated all men because he thought they would be just like his father. But, Jay Jay turned out to be really cool. Michael enjoyed running around in the back yard. There were no back yards where he came from to go play. For the first time, he enjoyed being a kid. After a day of football with Jay Jay, Michael would sit by the bedroom door where his mother was locked in. He heard her cry and talk to herself. His heart ached he couldn't stand hearing his mother cry. "Don't cry mommy. I'm here for you. I love you. You can do this mommy." He started to cry.

"Don't touch me. Don't touch me, Brian. Leave me alone." Rachel yelled. "Mommy, I'm here. I'm here." Michael yelled through the door.

Rachel heard his voice and snapped back into reality. She was flashing back to her rape from her Uncle Brian. She wiped the tears from her face and walked over to the door and sat down next to it. She placed her hand on the door as if Michael could feel her through it. "Mommy, are you okay?" Michael asked sniffling.

It amazed Rachel how much her baby had grew up and how he always tried to be her protector. It also hurt her because she knew he had grown up before his time. She swallowed the saliva in her mouth. "I'm okay baby. Don't cry. Mommy was remembering what happened to me when I was pregnant with you."

"Why do you and Janet always cry and scream at night?" Michael asked.

Rachel got quiet. She had no idea that Janet still had nightmare about what Brian did to them. She was going to have to talk to Janet about that. "Baby, I'll tell you about that later. I don't know if you will understand."

"I'll understand mommy." Michael

said slowly.

"Well okay. Just don't say anything to Janet. Brian was our uncle. He lived at Momma's house when both of us were left there by our parents. He was a bad man. He used to hurt us a lot. In fact, all the kids that lived there. Remember when I told you to never let anyone touch your private parts? Well that was what our Uncle Brian did to us."

"I'll bite him mommy. I'll beat him up." Michael yelled while swinging his little fist with anger from what he just heard.

"He's no longer around or should I say alive. He's dead."

"How did he die, mommy?"

Rachel sat there nervously thinking back to that day as she stood in the alleyway and watched Black Ice pull out Brian's windpipe from his neck. "I'll tell you that part when you get older."

"Okay mommy."

They spent the rest of the night talking back and forth through the door. They did that every day until Rachel was better. Rachel started gaining her weight back and her skin cleared up. She started to look like the beautiful woman she was. Michael and Rachel spent every day talking.

Their relationship grew closer than it was before.

Janet stood by her cousin and helped her get stronger. All of them together were the happiest they have ever been. Rachel crept downstairs into the basement and went behind the stairs to where the duffle bags were. She opened the bag and took three stacks of money. Michael followed closely behind his mother without her knowing. They were getting so close lately that he didn't want to leave her side. "What are you doing?" Michael asked.

Rachel jumped from being startled by the sound of his voice. "Boy, don't be sneaking up on me like that. You hear me?" she said. Michael watched his mother take the money and zip back up the bag, but not before he got a chance to look in it. He saw the money and the shiny guns. "We're going shopping today." Rachel said with a big smile while grabbing his hand and leading him back up the stairs.

"Really mommy, we're going shopping?" Michael asked with excitement.

"Yes baby." She nodded.

Rachel, Michael, Janet and Jay Jay left and spent the day shopping in Sunrise Mall. They bought brand new clothes that all of them could carry. Michael was so happy that he was getting all these new clothes.

Chapter 28

Black Ice inhaled the cigarette smoke full of crack as he sat in his white Lexus on a block next to Kings Highway. He waited for Caesar and Ace to come and drop off his money. He started to think about Rachel and Michael and wondered where the hell they were at. It was well over a month. Then he started wondering where Roxy was too. He was going to kill them when he did find them. Black Ice looked down in his hand at the piece of paper he held. He found the paper in Rachel's jeans pocket at his apartment in Bedstuy. He read the 516 number over and over. That could only be a number in Long Island. Rachel doesn't have any friends there.

Bang! Bang! Bang! Black Ice thoughts were interrupted by his car being shredded up by bullets. Bullets whistled passed his head as he covered up close to the seat. He crawled to the passenger side and opened the door. He crawled out of the car down to the sidewalk. He pulled his 38 special-revolver from his waist and slowly pulled his head using his car for cover to see who was shooting at him. Bang! Bang! Bang! He sat back down low ducking his head and taking cover again from the shots being fired at him. Bang! A shot rang out hitting him in the side of his shoulder tearing through his flesh knocking him over. Black Ice quickly aimed his gun at the direction the shot came from while lying on his back. Black Ice was shocked. He saw Caesar running towards him firing off shots from a 45 handgun. Black Ice snapped out of shock. "You mother fucker!" He yelled while squeezing the trigger of his 38 special. A shot went flying by Caesar's head making him duck low and take cover. Caesar returned fire. Black Ice jumped up to his feet while firing his gun. He thought if Caesar was firing at him from the side then who was shooting from across the street. As soon as that thought ran through his mind, Ace was seen trying to sneak up on him. Black Ice quickly tried to grab another gun. He realized he only had the 38 special that only held six bullets. No way in hell thought that he would need a gun today. He was only coming to pick up money from Caesar and Ace. He picked the meeting place and only brought the 38 special because he never left the house without a gun on him. Black Ice knew he had to think fast. He only had two more shots left and

Ace and Caesar were closing in on him. Black Ice rose and fired. One shot and took off running.

"Don't let him get away!" Caesar yelled at Ace while he ran after Black Ice. Ace was firing wildly and crazy at Black Ice. Black Ice looked back to see Ace and Caesar chasing him and shook his head. He ducked low while running in between cars. Bang! Bang! Bang! Caesar 45 and Ace's 9mm guns went off simultaneously. A shot his Black Ice in the back as he tumbled down to the ground. He rolled and got right back up.

"Shit, that nigga is still moving." Ace screamed out of breath from running.

"I don't know, but we got to make sure he dies." Caesar replied while still firing at Black Ice. Another shot hit Black Ice in his shoulder.

Black Ice continued running thinking he just needs to make it to a main road. That pussy won't fire at me in front of people. He ran, but began to slow down. His body felt weak from losing blood.

"Look. Look he's starting to slow down." Bang! Bang Bang! The bullet entered his butt cheeks and Black Ice collapsed down to the sidewalk.

Ace and Caesar began to run faster to get to Black Ice's body to make sure they finished the job. They heard police sirens and two cars pulled up and the cops jumped out of their cars. They started to fire and Ace and Caesar.

"Aw shit!" Caesar hollered while exchanging fire right back at the cops. The cops ran behind their cars. Ace and Caesar took off running down the block firing back over their shoulders to keep the cops from following them. They ran through the back yard of a house on the block and hopped a fence and ran towards Caesar's car that was parked. They hopped in the car and pulled off slowly and a cop car passed them.

Black Ice felt the blood making his clothes feel soaked. He dropped the gun and kicked it while lying on the ground feeling like he was bleeding to death. He opened his eyes to see four white cops standing over him. All he could think of, was that is the second time I was saved by a bunch of cops from being killed as he passed out from the loss of blood and lost consciousness.

Chapter 29

Black Ice slowly opened his eyes, but it was painful and hard to do. It felt as if his eyelids weighed a ton. He tried to swallow, but he couldn't he felt pain every time he tried. He realized that there was something stuck in his throat. He focused his eyes to see a tube jammed down his throat and nose. He moved his right hand to pull out a clear tube that was stuck in his hand. But he couldn't move his hand as he was handcuffed to the bed rail. He moved his hand around to only here the clanging sound of metal on metal. "What the fuck was going on?" Black Ice tried to say with a tube down his throat. He tried to figure out where he was and how he got there. Flashbacks started to come to his mind at once. He could see Caesar and Ace running after him shooting and then.

"I see you're up." A deep voice said breaking Black Ice's thought. He looked up at the door to see a man standing in the doorway. He knew that face well. The man walked closer and leaned down in his face. "I finally got your black ass." Detective Roy said while staring into Black Ice's cold eyes. "You've done fucked up you son of a bitch.

And I'm going to make sure you end up on death row. I know it was you that cut out James's eyes and tongue. That's a fucked up way to leave a man. You could of finished the job and kill him, but you wanted to live life and walk around that way. I also know the pair of hands that were thrown over a power line was the doing of you. I bet you even those niggas that were trying to hit on you five weeks ago has something to do with your ass.

Black Ice eyes opened wide and he tried to mumble the words 'five weeks'.

"Oh you don't know do you? Well your ass has been in a coma for a week from the blood loss from the bullet wounds you received. I'll kill you myself, but there are too many eyes on you right now. My boss wants you alive. See we can't prove you murdered those two cops in the projects. You made sure of that." Detective Roy said sarcastically. "See we don't care when your ass go around killing your own fucking kind, but when you start killing white people and cops then you are going to have a fucking problem."

Black Ice looked at the detective and a grin crossed his face.

"You think this shit is funny?" Detective

178

Roy yelled as he became furious and his face turned bright red. "We'll see how funny you'll like this. See you left one of your half smoked special cigarettes on the ground of Officer Reed's house when you murdered him and his family. You stupid mother fucker, do you know when we found them? It was four days later."

Black Ice tried to laugh, but his throat was too sore. He knew the only reason Detective Roy was so mad was because it was a white baby.

"What the fuck? You still think this shit is funny? Well, Office Reed was missing his work bag when we searched his house. On the day the officer's found you ass dying on the ground, they didn't know who you were at the time. If they did, I'm pretty sure they would have let your ass die right there on the ground. But on that day, you had a bulletproof vest on that saved your life. All together there were fourteen bullets in the vest, but you got shot in both shoulders and your lower back. The bullet hit you liver. Oh and you got shot in your ass. Those boys were really trying to kill your ass." Detective Roy said with a smile. "But, what really made my day was the bulletproof vest you had on had a name stitched in it. All officers have to have the name sewn into their vest. The one that you were wearing was Officer Reed's. That was the proof I needed to put your ass in the house and proof enough to get a warrant to take your D.N.A. to match it to the cigarette you left next to Reed's body. I got your ass now."

Black Ice knew he was fucked. How could I leave a cigarette butt there he thought. The crack had him slipping. How did these fools Ace and Caesar tried to kill him.

Detective Roy saw the anger on Black Ice's face and he smiled inside. "Oh yeah you have been here for a while. The doctor is going to test your blood one more time and then I'll move you tomorrow to jail. You're going to spend the rest of your life in a cell, asshole. And don't think about escaping." Detective Roy said walking out the room and then a mean looking cop stepped in the room. Detective Roy just then turned around and said, "See Joe here doesn't like you, none of us like cop killers and he has the order to shoot you if you ever look at him wrong in anyway." Office Joe looked at Black Ice and the eyes thought he was going to give Black Ice a reason to look

180

at him wrong just to shoot him or hurt him by giving him an ass whooping he never had. Office Joe just smiled at the thought of the sure pleasure of doing so. Black Ice laid there pissed off. He just thought that if he ever got out of there he was going to kill Ace and Caesar.

Later that day, Black Ice watched as an elderly black woman entered the room. "I'm your nurse sugar and I have to draw blood. The doctor wants to test it to make sure you're all right. I'm sure you are though. When you came here, you weighed less than me. But you got your weight back. We've been feeding you through that tube in your mouth. As a matter of fact, you don't need those anymore." She said as she pulled the tubes out. "See doesn't that feel better? There should be someone coming in to drop off you dinner soon. I don't know if what those people are saying about you is true, but I hope not. We don't need any more black men in this world making us look like bad people. But they damn sure have had that police office outside your door." She said.

There was a small tray that was by the nurse's side with needle syringes and cleaning pads on it. She turned her head to reach for the drawer reaching for some latex gloves. She turned back to grab a syringe and there wasn't anything there. She could have sworn she put four syringes on the tray, but she only saw two. She looked at Black Ice suspiciously.

Black Ice just stared at the woman like she had lost her mind. She felt exactly like she lost her mind. "Please give me your left arm." She asked. Black Ice didn't realize that his arm was loose from the handcuff to the bed rail. He was too busy thinking about ways to kill Ace and Caesar. He raised his arm like the nurse told him to do. "You don't have to worry about me sticking you with the needle. You see that thing in your arm is an IV. It's already threaded through your vein in your arm. I'm going to draw blood from your IV and it won't hurt a bit. You see I have to push the air out of the syringe. If I was to push air in the vein, a person would die from a heart attack."

Black Ice thought this bitch talked too much as she was drawing his blood and filling the tubes with blood. Once she was done, she left the room. He thought the bitch would never shut up and leave. He started to think how he was going to get out of the hospital. He tried to wiggle the handcuffs, but from the noise Officer Joe and the doctor entered the room.

"Don't think you are going to escape boy."

Black Ice laughed, "Who are you calling a boy? All you pigs are the same. You think your tough until I put a knife in your gut and have you bleeding like I did your little friend."

Officer Joe turned bright red full of anger and clenched and unclenching his fists. Black Ice saw the color of his face and knew he was getting to him. He decided to keep pushing his buttons. "You should have seen the bullets I shot tore through those cops' heads in the projects. I bet they had a closed coffin funeral."

"You asshole" Officer Joe ran to Black Ice's hospital bed. He swung and hit Black Ice in the jaw and repeatedly punched him over and over. "I'll kill you. You'll never make it to jail." Joe laid each punch to Black Ice's face. The blood was dripping out his mouth. Joe was so busy in his rage he never noticed that Black Ice wasn't using his left hand that was free to cover his face to protect himself. He felt around with his left arm on the bed for the syringes he stole off the nurse's tray. He gripped them tight and did his best to jab Joe with them. But for every punch that Joe struck his face, made it even harder for him to have the strength to strike Joe with the syringes. Black Ice got the urge to swing and hit Officer Joe in the neck with the syringe and pressed down on the syringe at the same time. Officer Joe stepped back to pull the needle out of his neck and reached for his gun. Black Ice noticed he missed the spot he was aiming for. His heart began to pound. He grabbed the other syringe and swung it with all his might hitting Officer Joe in the neck just as he raised his gun and pointed it at Black Ice's head. Black Ice pressed down on the syringe. The air from the syringe rushed through Officer Joe's vein. He dropped his gun as he felt his heart tighten. He clenched his chest and gasped for air. His eyes rolled to the back of his head as he collapsed to the floor. Black Ice watched his chest go up and down really fast until it quit moving at all. Black Ice reached for Officer Joe's keys with his foot over the bed. He got a hold of them with his toes and slowly raised them up for his reach. He scrambled threw the keys with his left hand. He removes the handcuff's himself from the bed rails. He was happy was free as he rubbed his wrist and ankles. He bent over to see if Officer Joe was still breathing. He felt air coming out of his nose. He thought, 'shit that old bitch wasn't lying when she said that shit' when the elderly nurse was in earlier that day to take his blood. He smiled to himself and stole the two syringes that the nurse mistakenly left in the room. He then thought how he was going to get out of the hospital. He looked down and realized that he didn't have any clothes, just the green hospital gown. He picked up the gun off the floor and pushed Officer Joe's body up under the bed.

Just then his door opened half way; he quickly jumped back in the bed. "It's dinner time." A man said as he entered the room carrying a tray of food and placed it on the table and wheeled it over next to the bed. "It's not the best food in the world, but it's good." He said to Black Ice. The hospital worked turned towards the bed as Black Ice got out of bed and raised the 9mm gun and placed it up against the back of the man's head. "Don't say a fucking work or I'll blow your fucking brains out." Black Ice said. The man shook his head wanting to say yes, but too afraid to talk.

"Get undressed." Black Ice said. The man hurried getting undressed quickly out of his scrubs.

Two minutes later, Black Ice stepped out of the room fully dressed in the man's scrubs and walked down the hospital hallway. No one paid him any attention as to who just walked out of the room or who he was. He saw the exit door for the stairs and ran down them, through the lobby, and out the front door of the hospital, a free man.

Chapter 30

Detective Roy came to the hospital bright and early the next day with a uniform cop following closely behind him. He walked down the hallway feeling great with a grin creasing his face from ear to ear. It was going to be a good old day he thought. He was finally going to put Black Ice away for the rest of his life.

They stopped in front of Black Ice's hospital room noticing an empty chair where Officer Joe was supposed to be guarding the door. Detective Roy looked at the other cop and said, "Tim, where is Joe?"

"He most likely went down to the cafeteria to grab a doughnut and some coffee." Tim replied.

"I gave his strict orders for him to not leave this area and to remain guarding this door."

Detective Roy felt his stomach tightening and knew something was wrong. He pulled his 9mm gun out of his holster and pushed the door open. He looked at the bed and could see Black Ice lying there with the sheet covering his head. He took a sigh of relief and put his gun back in the holster. As he walked up to the bed and said, "You sleep good asshole? I hope so because this is going to be the last day you live somewhat under normal conditions without being surrounded by bars." Detective Roy laughed and his belly shook. He suddenly stopped laughing when Black Ice didn't answer him. He looked down at the sheets and stopped short in shock. The bed sheets were covered in blood and looked to see blood was pouring from his neck. "No! No! You're not going to get out of this that easy." He put his hands over the wound to cover it. When he pulled the sheets from the head, he looked to see it wasn't Black Ice. He yelled for the other cop as he removed his hands from the dead man's neck. Detective Roy's foot hit something under the bed. He looked down to see Officer Joe's dead body.

"Shut down the hospital! Cover all exits of this building. We can't let Black Ice escape!" Detective Roy hollered his orders. The other cop used his radio to call for back up. Little did both of them know that Black Ice was long gone!

Chapter 31

Life was going great for Caesar and
Ace. They had control of the business.
Everything that came in and out of
Brownsville Projects was their doing. They
knew that Black Ice was in the hospital and
the cops were watching him twenty four
hours a day. And soon they would be taking
him to jail for life. They had nothing to fear
or so they thought. They didn't have to live
up to their promise to J-Rock and Smoke.
Black Ice had cut out J-Rock's eyes and
tongue and Smoke's body had yet to turn up.
Ace drove down the block and
stopped in front of a two story house. He
hopped out of the car with Lisa behind him.
"This is it baby. This is your house. Your
name is on the papers." Ace said to Lisa
proudly.
"Oh my God, oh my God I love you
daddy." Lisa hugged Ace in excitement as
she jumped into his arms.
"Come on let's go inside." Ace
opened the back door of his car and got his
two sons' out. They all walked up to the
house. "Lisa, take the keys out of my
pocket."
Lisa dug deep down in his pocket and

189

pulled out a set of keys. She put the key into the door lock and opened the door. They all entered the house. "Damn baby. It's so big. When do we get to move in?" Lisa asked.

"Today boo, today. We're going to go shopping so you hook the place up. Are you happy with it?" Ace asked Lisa.

"I'm more than happy." Lisa said as she kissed him passionately and deeply.

Chapter 32

"Yea suck it" As he moaned while watching her suck his dick slowly with long strokes making her way up and down his shaft. 'Damn this bitch is a freak' he thought to himself. She looked up into his eyes as she slurped in and out. She picked up her pace moving up and down his dick moving faster with each stroked going deep back in her throat swallowing the excess saliva that was building up in her mouth. "Shit girl. I'm going to cum." He yelled as he busted a nut in her mouth as she moaned still sucking his dick and swallowing every last drop of cum making him shiver from the sensation. "Shit girl. You got me feeling all weak.

Lisa licked her lips with a lustful smile. "When the fuck are you going to tell Ace and take me away from him Caesar?"

Caesar looked at Lisa from the corner of his eye and zipped up his pants. "Damn here you go with that shit again." He said.

"Listen Caesar, I'm tired of his ass and if you don't tell him soon, I will." Lisa said while rolling her neck. "I want to be free. I want to be with you." She said and leaned over and nibbled on his ear.

Caesar wasn't a fool like Ace. He knew Lisa was a scandalous bitch and the only reason she wanted out of her relationship with Ace was so she could run wild in the streets and leave her kids at home making Shelly watch them. "Bitch I ain't telling him yet. I'll tell him when I'm ready. You're only acting up because that nigga won't let you run the streets all crazy like your hot ass wants too." Caesar said.

"So what if I want to go out and do me. This is my pussy, not yours. And I can give it up to whomever I want to." Lisa snapped back.

Caesar back slapped her across the face. "Listen as long as you are the mother of my child, you won't be running the streets whoring, that pussy out." Caesar hollered. "You're just mad that Ace feels the same way. That nigga takes good care of your slut ass. He just brought you that house in Sheepshead Bay."

"Fuck you and him, Caesar!" Lisa said while rubbing her cheek. "If you don't tell him soon, I'm going to tell him."

"Calm the fuck down. I'll tell him soon as I'm ready. Right now, we're making too much money to fuck up our business and friendship over your pussy. Lisa, let's keep it real. You know you're with him for the money and me too. And if you open up your big mouth before I get everything straight, your ass will be out on the street with no place to live or no money because you want to mess it up. Do you understand?" Caesar asked.

Caesar saw Lisa's eyes and knew his words got her to thinking. Lisa didn't want to go back to the projects and knew Caesar was right. She and Ace would start fighting and she would lose her house and the money. She wanted to run the streets, not live on them. "All right, Caesar. I'll do it your way for now." She got up out of the car and slammed the car door. She walked around the corner up to her new house Ace just bought her. Caesar pulled off shaking his head thinking that he had to do something to that bitch, but headed home thinking of the pussy he was going to go home to and that he really wanted.

Chapter 33

    Ace pulled up to his house as soon as the sun begun to rise. It was a long night watching the block and making sure those young niggas were hustling as he counted the money. He got out of his car and shut and locked the door. A thousand things were running through Ace's mind as he made his way to the front door of their new house. Every time he called Lisa that bitch wouldn't answer. He even called at ten o'clock p.m. and kept trying for an hour straight still no answer. He even tried to call Caesar at ten o'clock too and he didn't even answer. But soon as eleven thirty came around Lisa picked up the phone and then Caesar called him back. He never understood why he couldn't get those two at the same time when he was out working.

    Ace was wondering why his mind was tripping by putting thoughts in his head, but something didn't feel right. Ace entered the house. He made up his mind that he was going to ask Lisa what she was doing last night. She was probably sleeping that's all. He just needed to believe that. She wouldn't mess with my men. She was a good woman and loved Ace. He was the one out there all day or night long making the money. She probably thinks he's out there fucking. He just needed to stop thinking because he didn't want to push Lisa away by being paranoid.

When he walked in the door, he could hear moans in the bedroom. He ran back to the bedroom and opened the door and yelled, "Lisa, what the fuck are you doing?"

He jumped back in shock as he watched Lisa hanging from the ceiling by a rope on her feet. Her whole body was wrapped with the rope. Ace pulled out his 9mm and looked around and didn't see any one. "Baby, what happened?" he asked Lisa.

Just then the door shut behind him and Black Ice stepped from behind it and put the barrel of his 44 revolver to Ace's head and said, "Hey Ace."

Ace's body went in shock as he felt a chill run down his spine. He knew that voice to well and he knew his life would soon be over. "Ace, drop the fucking gun and go stand next to your bitch" Black Ice said. Ace dropped the gun and walked over next to Lisa who was still hanging in the air. He turned around and looked into black Ice's eyes. "He….he….hurt our babies, I

195

heard them screaming." Lisa said to Ace crying. "He came in here from their room with blood all over his hands."

Ace felt pain in his heart and stomach and wanted to rush Black Ice with everything he had. "You hurt my children?" Ace yelled with tears in his eyes.

"No, Ace I didn't hurt your boy. Now, shut the fuck up. See I know you would have never crossed me without someone putting thoughts in your head. So, I blame your bitch and Caesar." Black Ice said.

Ace swallowed. He knew what Black Ice said was true. "But, that doesn't mean I'm not going to kill you. I was going to kill Lisa, but she deserves something worse than death. Scandalous bitches like her always do. I made her smoke crack all night and you already know what that means." Black Ice started getting in to Ace's head.

Ace looked at Lisa's face that was upside down and could see the glassy look in her eyes. "Why did you do that, why?" Ace asked.

"Because that bitch is a slut, tell him how long you have been fucking Caesar." Black Ice said to Lisa.

Ace felt as his heart was about to be

196

crushed. "Talk bitch or I will put a bullet in your head." He said to Lisa.

Lisa sniffed and said, "I have been fucking with Caesar for three years. I'm sorry baby. I'm so sorry."

"What the fuck you mean you're sorry? Your sorry you been fucking my man for three years?" Ace said and punched Lisa in the ribs. He punched her over and over out of rage. Lisa cried in pain trying to apologize to Ace.

"Yo, that's not the best part. I watched this bitch give him head last night in his car and then followed her to the house. And then we have been getting to know each other really well. That bitch fucked me and told me where you stashed your money bags. She told me it was you and Caesar's idea to kill me and then begged me not to kill her. Tell him bitch. Tell him what I want you to tell him." Black Ice said to Lisa.

"No. No. He'll fuck me up." Lisa said.

"Bitch, if you don't tell him. I'll fuck you up." He said.

Ace looked back and forth at Black Ice and Lisa wondering what else they could say to break his heart even more. There

197

wasn't too much more he could take. He wanted Black Ice to kill him so the pain in his heart would stop.

"Talk bitch." Black Ice demanded.

Lisa cried and said, "Our youngest son, Mark, ain't your son. He's Caesar's son."

"What!" Ace yelled not believing what he just had heard. "No."

"That not your son. I just lied to you." Lisa cried.

Ace now understood when Caesar would buy things for Mark and not Ace's other son. Ace's mind flashed back to the day his son was born. Caesar was there and was just as happy as Ace was or even more. It was all coming clear now. A stream of tears ran down his Ace's face. 'No! No!' he moaned as he buried his face in his hands.

Black Ice leaned his head back and started to laugh and enjoying Ace's pain. In a blink of an eye, Ace dove for his 9 mm on the floor. Black Ice stopped laughing as soon as he saw what Ace was doing, but it was too late. The gun was already in Ace's hand. Black Ice squeezed the trigger of the 44 bulldog revolver. The bullet tore into Ace's stomach knocking him back, but not off his feet. Black Ice fired two more shots hitting Ace in the chest. Ace gasped for air and dropped down to the floor clenching his chest. Blood was pouring out of his mouth. Black Ice watched as Ace choked on his own blood.

Ace rose his 9mm. Black Ice was about to shoot him again, but was surprised at what he saw. Ace wasn't pointing the gun at him. Ace was pointing the loaded 9 mm gun towards Lisa's temple. Lisa tried to wiggle, but was stuck upside down in the air. She watched Ace cough up. "No!" Lisa yelled as he pulled the trigger twice. The bullets pierced her skull sending pieces of skull and brain flying all over the room. He made a gasping sound and collapsed dead on the floor.

Black Ice thought that was some shit like it was a scene from a movie right in front of his eyes. He regretted taking his eyes off Ace. He wanted to make Lisa a crack head as death was too good for her. He put his gun back in his waist band and walked out of the bedroom with a bag full of Ace's money and walked into the children's room and came out with another bag. Black Ice walked out of the house heading for his next victim.

Chapter 34

Detective Roy pulled up to the crime scene. He heard it on the radio and knew it could only be the work of Black Ice. He had an A.P.B. out on Black Ice so every cop in the city was looking for him. And here he was back in Brooklyn. Detective Roy steeped out of his black Crown Victoria and looked at all the uniform cops surrounding the house. Detective Roy flashed his badge and made his way up to the house. At the door he met a uniform cop name, Bob, who was in charge of the crime scene. "Hi, how are you doing detective?"

"I'll be better once I get the bastard that did this." Detective Roy replied.

"Do you think it's the same guy you are looking for?" Bob asked.

"We'll see." Roy replied. They walked in the door. "Shit this is a nice house." Roy said out loud not meaning too.

"Yea, it's nice what you can get with drug money." Bob replied. Bob walked him through the living room. Roy saw a young black lady officer consoling a young boy, not more than five years old. Roy looked at the boy in the lady's arms who was crying and kept repeating, "I saw him! I saw him doing it!" The little boy kept repeating those words in between breaths and tears. Roy knew it was the victim's son as he walked back to the master bedroom.

"Shit!" he yelled as he saw the bodies still in the same place while the officers were collecting evidence. He walked in and looked at the woman hanging by her feet from the ceiling with her had blown in half and pieces of brain were scattered all over the floor. He looked down at the dead man. "I need to turn him over." Detective Roy said to the officers.

"Okay. I think they got most of the evidence." Bob replied.

Detective Roy put on some clear gloves and bent down to turn over the body. He looked at the hole in the man's chest then his face. "This is one of Black Ice's men. So this here has to be his work.

"There is something else I have to show you. Follow me." Bob said.

Roy followed Bob into a room that looked like the children's room. He entered the room and looked in the middle of the floor and began to vomit at the sight of what he saw. Roy ran out of the room, through the house, and out the door. Bob followed him out of the house.

"Shit that monster." Roy yelled. His hands shook as he couldn't believe what he saw. He reached into his pocket to pull out a cigarette and lit it.

"I know how you feel. I did the same thing when I first saw it too." Bob put his hand on Roy's shoulder.

"That was not human like. He's a monster." Roy said.

Detective Roy began to think of that dead man's name. He arrested him once. "I got to go back to the precinct and look up some information. Thank you for your help Bob. I think I got a lead that I have to follow."

"Alright, I'm glad I could help you in any way. I hope you find this animal. The boys and I are on standby whenever you need us." Bob said to Roy. Roy jumped back into his black Crown Victoria and pulled off.

Chapter 35

Black Ice couldn't believe how easy it was to pick the lock on the door. He slowly opened it and quietly entered. He gently shut the door. He pulled out his 44 bulldog revolver and held the black bag over his shoulder. He made his way through the apartment. Black Ice could hear the sounds of love making. The moans and groans grew louder and louder as he made his way closer to the bedroom.

"Yes daddy! Yes! Fuck me. I….I...love…you." The voice of a woman moaned.

Black Ice could hear the woman's voice. It was a voice that was very familiar to him. He slowly pushed the door open and watched the man's back that was turned to him pound and hump away at a woman from the back. Black Ice felt a déjà vu moment as he kept watching. His body stood paralyzed at what he saw. His heart began to race and could feel the rage rise from his toes to his head. He walked over to the bed and smacked Caesar with the butt of the revolver sending him flying to the floor. Caesar laid there in pain while holding his head.

The woman looked back to see what

happened and what she saw sent chills down her spine as she broke down in tears.

"Bitch, why is it every time I find you your ass is up in the air? All this time I have been looking for you and you have been here with this fool? I see you're not smoking crack as much as you used too. You got thicker Roxy." Black Ice said with his devilish smile.

Roxy looked in Black Ice's eyes and all what felt was coming back to normal in her life was just draining out of her body. Black Ice faced Caesar and said, "You grim mother fucker. So, you are behind my woman? Is this why I couldn't find her? You did always want Roxy, but she never wanted your ass. So, you took her when she was weak. Its ok my friend. You can never keep your dick in your pants." Black Ice said.

Caesar removed his hands from his head and looked at the blood. He knew he needed to reach for his gun up under the bed or he surely was going to be a dead man. "It was Ace's idea to cross you and that bitch, Roxy, came on to me." Caesar lied.

That night that Black Ice killed those two men over at Roxy's apartment and Caesar and Ace had to clean the mess up and get rid of the bodies in the ocean. Caesar dropped Ace off and went back to Roxy's apartment and talked to her. He promised her that he would hide her and take care of her. So, he moved her in his apartment and one thing led to another. Then they became lovers. She slowed down on smoking crack, but she still got high just not as much.

Roxy couldn't believe what she heard Caesar say. She knew Caesar was afraid of Black Ice like everyone else, but not a punk. Now she knew he was.

"Fool shut the fuck up. Roxy only did it because she was scared of me and thought like a fool that you would protect her." Black Ice laughed.

Caesar tried to ease his hand under the bed to reach for his gun. Black Ice jumped on him and began pounding him with blow after blow to the head. "You think I'm stupid?" Black Ice hollered.

Those words were the last words Caesar heard before he lost consciousness from Black Ice's beating to his head. Black Ice looked at Caesar. He put his hand under the bed and pulled out the 45 handgun Caesar was trying to reach. He got up and turned towards Roxy.

Roxy was crying and lying on the bed

covered with a sheet. She was still there to Black Ice's surprise. "Why didn't you try to run?" Black Ice asked in a confused tone.

"What's the point? You'll just find me again." Roxy said in between tears.

"Well your right about one thing. There is no point of running because I will get you. But, you don't have to worry about me trying to find you again." Black Ice raised the 45 handgun he found under the bed and pointed it at Roxy.

"Wait, wait…..I'm carrying your baby." Roxy yelled.

"No one is carrying my baby." Black Ice said and pulled the trigger twice. The first bullet entered Roxy's chest knocking her back in to the head board of the bed. The second bullet entered her head and she slumped over dead. Without any hesitation, Black Ice tied up Caesar's body and hauled him to his car and took off.

A half an hour later, Caesar woke up and couldn't move. He looked around and his hands were tied and his knees were tied up to his chest. His body was stuck in a small spot. He saw Black Ice looking down on him. "I see you are up. You cross the wrong mother fucker and now you're going to pay. Oh yea. I stopped and paid a visit at

Ace's house." Black Ice snickered.

All Caesar could do was think of his son and hoped that he was all right. "I'm going to throw you in the ocean Caesar. You will die slowly like a rat that you are. It will give you plenty of time to think. Oh yea. There's a knife, flash light and a few other things in this bag for you to buy your time." Black Ice said as he thru the bag in the barrel with Caesar. Black Ice lifted the barrel lid and put it on top of the barrel.

Everything went dark for Caesar. He tried to move, but couldn't there was no room. He squirmed around since he was tied up. He felt the barrel fall over and roll, bumping him over and over until he heard a splash.

Black Ice watched the barrel sink deep into the Coney Island Ocean and smiled. He got in the car and pulled off.

Caesar began to panic not knowing what to do it was pitch black. He couldn't see his hand in front of his face. He felt for the bag that Black Ice threw in there with him. He found the opening of the bag and felt around inside of it. He felt something like rubber and wet. He felt the knife and the flash light.

He felt the barrel hit the bottom of the

ocean. He turned on the flashlight. His hands and arms were covered in blood. He calmed down and realized it wasn't his blood. He looked around and knew he was fucked. His legs hurt from being stuck so close to his body. He looked to see where the blood was coming from. It wasn't coming from him. He also wanted to see if there was something in the bag to help him break out of the barrel. Then he thought if there was something he'd probably die trying to swim to the top. But, he had to try to do something. He reached in the bag and again felt wetness. He pulled out something that felt like rubber. His eyes grew wider as he held what looked like a child's arm with his hand still attached to it. "What the fuck?" He dropped the arm and it fell on him with no other place to go. He again reached in the bag and felt something that felt like a rock. He put the flash light down and put his other hand in the bag. He pulled out the hard object. "AHHHHHHHH!!" Caesar screamed and screamed as tears streamed down his face. He screamed for 15 minutes straight until the batteries in the flash light died. He continued to scream in the dark with the object on his knees with no other place to go. The last thing he would

see was his son's head with his eyes opened
looking at him.

Chapter 36

Detective Roy was on his way to
Caesar's apartment on Pennsylvania Avenue
in Brooklyn until he heard a call on the
police radio, "Shot's fired. Shots fired at
1324 Pennsylvania Avenue."
"Shit that is where I'm heading. Damn."
Detective Roy said and stepped his foot hard
on the gas pedal. He turned the sirens on.
He prayed he wasn't too late to catch Black
Ice. He pulled up to the four story
apartment building. He hopped out of his
car. There were uniformed cops coming in
and out of the building. Detective Roy
walked up to one that was at the door.
"What do we have here?" he asked while
flashing his badge.
"Well sir, it looks like someone broke
into an apartment and shot a lady twice.
"What? Were there any men in the
apartment?"
"No sir, but the neighbors said they
heard voices of two men screaming before
the shots went off, but that's all we can get
out of them. We know that apartment is in
the name of Caesar Rosse. There was some
crack, some paraphernalia, and a few guns."
"Okay. What about the woman?"

"She was rushed to Brookdale Hospital. She was unable to talk. I don't think she'll make it. Man, I wonder what kind of a person would shoot a pregnant woman."

"What was she pregnant?"

"Yes about eight months pregnant."

"What was her name?" Detective Roy asked while pulling out a pad and a pen from his coat pocket.

"Roxy Walker."

"Thank you officer" Detective Roy said as he walked away.

He hopped back in his car and pulled out a cigarette. It wasn't a man that shot a pregnant woman. It was the devil he thought as he pulled off. His stomach tightened up as he remembered what he saw at Ace's house in the children's bedroom. There was a child of a three year old body that was missing his head and an arm. The voice of the five year old little boy that was left alive in the house saying repeatedly that he saw the man do it rang in Detective Roy's mind. He knew now what the little boy saw. He saw Black Ice chopping his little brother up in pieces.

Detective Roy headed to Brookdale Hospital in hopes to find another lead to

Black Ice. Still the voice of the little boy
kept ringing in his ears and made him feel
sick to his stomach.

Chapter 37

Michael has never been so happy in his life. Everything was going right for once. He got to feel what it felt like to be a normal child. He and his mother Rachel and her cousin Janet with her boyfriend spent the day at the movies in the mall. "Damn it's been a good day." Rachel said as she entered the house with Michael on her side followed by Jane and Jay Jay.

"Come on little man. Let's go watch some TV while the women cook." Jay Jay said to Michael.

"Oh yea, well tomorrow is the day for the men to cook. I just hope you don't burn the hot dogs." Janet said. And Rachel and Janet burst out laughing followed by Jay Jay and Michael's.
Michael and Jay Jay walked to the living room and plopped down on the couch and turned on the TV. They flicked through some channels until they found a movie.

Rachel was putting the butter on the rice and staring at it and said, "Janet I have to thank you. You saved our lives more than you know."

"Rachel, you don't have to thank me. We're family and you saved yourself.

Changes come from within and you changed you." Janet replied.

"But, still thank you. I needed to get away and you were there for me." Rachel said while tears rolled down her face. She tried her best to hold them in.

Janet walked over to her cousin and gave her a big hug. Rachel hugged her back and they just held each other for a while.

"Rachel I never told you, but I know you and Black Ice had something to do with Brian being killed. I'm glad it happened because I still have nightmares of what he did to me."

"Well it's over now, Janet. He'll never touch you again. Come on girl. Let's finish cooking so we can feed these boys. Shit we're in here getting all emotional." Rachel said and the both giggled and started cooking again.

A half an hour later, dinner was served on the table. They all sat down and prepared to start to eat. "Hold up let say a prayer." Rachel said. They all folded their hands, closed their eyes, and bowed their heads. Michael squeezed his mother's hand tight and loving. "God, Thank you for the many blessing you have given us and for keeping us strong when we felt weak. I beg and ask you that you continue to bless us with you grace. Thank you for this wonderful meal. Amen."

"Amen." They all said in unison.

Michael watched every one for a minute and began to eat. He finally felt as if he was part of a family.

"Janet, I'm thinking of taking some of the money I have and put a down payment on a house around here. I like it out here. Would you help me?" Rachel asked.

"Of course girl, you didn't have to ask and it's about time. If you're ready, I'd really like for you and Michael to stay and live with me. It makes the house feel as if it has more love in it. Michael grinned from ear to ear hearing the news.

"I also want to go back to school. I need you to help me with that too." Rachel continued.

"Not a problem Rachel." Janet replied as she was stuffing her mouth. Just then the doorbell rang several times in a row.
"Damn, who could that be at the door at this hour? Jay Jay, baby, do you mind answering the door for me?" Janet asked.

"Not at all, baby." Jay Jay stood up and left the dining room and headed for the front door. He opened the door. "Yea, can I help you?" Jay Jay said.

Back at the dining room, Janet continued her conversation with Rachel. "Yea, Rachel there are some good schools out here for you and Michael."

"I can't wait to get started and get my life back on track." Rachel said. Michael watched the two women talk while he ate his chicken and swung his feet that couldn't reach to the floor yet.

"Damn, I wonder what's taking that man so long to answer the door." Janet asked about Jay Jay.

Just then Jay Jay entered the dining room. "Baby, what took you so long? Your food is getting cold. Who was at the door?" Janet asked as Rachel and Michael watched Jay Jay and wanted to know too. Rachel noticed Jay Jay's jeans were wet right at his crotch area. The stench of urine made its way through the house. "Baby, did you pee on yourself?" Janet asked looking down at his crotch then back up to his face. She noticed his face was covered in sweat. Jay Jay didn't say a word.

"Well, well, well..." A voice said coming out of the hall and entering the living room with the barrel of a gun pointed at Jay Jay's head. Chills ran down Rachel's spine as she knew that voice all too well. She looked up and fear was written all over her face.

"I see my family is doing well, hey Junior." Black Ice said looking at his son.

Michael's heart jumped out of his chest in fear and knew things would never be the same now. Michael looked at his father's cold dark eyes and matched his stare. "Go away daddy. Go away please."

"Shut the fuck up you little punk." Black Ice yelled.

"How….how did you…" Rachel was unable to get all the words out.

"How did I find you? Bitch, you left a number in your jean's pocket at the apartment. It was a 516 number and that didn't take me long to realize it was a Long Island number. And then this little bitch right here is in the yellow pages." Black Ice said while pointing to Janet. "You are fucking this fool, Rachel." Black Ice yelled as he stuck the barrel of the 44 bulldog revolver in the back of Jay Jay's head. "This fool ain't even a man. Look he pissed on himself." Just then Jay Jay felt the cold steal barrel on his head and his bowels emptied making the whole room stink. "No your ass didn't?" Black Ice yelled as the smell hit his nose. "Now you shit on yourself too?"

"Please man. Don't kill me." Jay Jay begged. He had heard stories from Janet and Rachel how easy Black Ice would take a life and he wanted no part of it. "Janet's my girl. I have never touched Rachel. Please let us go. We didn't do nothing wrong." He begged.

"Didn't I tell you to keep your punk ass mouth shut at the door?" Black Ice bent closer to Jay Jay's ear. "Guess you won't be touching Janet no more."

"What man, please." Jay Jay said as just then Black Ice squeezed the trigger and blew a hole in the back of Jay Jay's neck instantly severing his spinal cord killing him.

"Nooooo!" Janet yelled as she watched Jay Jay's lifeless body fall to the floor.

Black Ice quickly turned around and aimed the gun at Janet.

"Please no, no!" Rachel and Michael yelled while crying. They felt as they were to blame for such pain on the people that helped and loved them. Black Ice fired off another shot. The bullet slammed into Janet's shoulder. Janet lay on the floor crying.

Rachel moved quickly and grabbed a knife that was on the dining room table and ran up to Black Ice driving it hard into Black Ice's bicep. He screamed and hit Rachel in the face with the gun in his hand. Rachel went flying backwards holding onto her face in pain. She began to rush him again with the knife in her hand.

"Bitch if you don't put that knife down, I'm going to blow your cousins fucking brains out." Black Ice warned.

Rachel stopped short of stabbing him again and looked at the gun that he had pointed at Janet.

"Drop it Rachel. I'm not playing with your ass." He cocked the hammer of the gun back to show her he was serious. Rachel knew she couldn't live with herself if Black Ice killed her cousin. So she dropped the knife and began to cry.

Black Ice walked up to her and punched her in the eye. Rachel fell back by Janet on the floor. "You want to stab me, bitch?" Black Ice yelled as he kicked Rachel in the ribs. "I'll kill you and your cousin."

Rachel looked up between the kick she was receiving and saw a deranged look in Black Ice's eyes and she knew she wouldn't live to see another day. Black Ice's anger rose and he started kicking and stomping both Rachel and Janet viciously. The women's screams could be heard from blocks away, but little by little their voices started to die out and got weaker. They grabbed each other and hugged each other as Black Ice continued to ramp and rage. "Bitch, you wanted to disrespect me. I'm the man. I'm the man!" Black Ice yelled.

Bang! A gun shot fired off hitting Black Ice in the back and knocking him forward. He grabbed a chair to keep him from falling over. He stood up straight and turned around. He was met by a pair of cold dark eyes like his very own, but in the form of a seven year old.

Michael held the chrome sub nose 3.8 revolver tightly and kept it pointed at his father. While Black Ice was beating Rachel and Janet, Michael couldn't cry anymore. He had crept down to the basement and went to the hiding place that he followed his mother to one day. He grabbed one of the guns and ran back upstairs in hopes to stop his father from killing the people he loved. "Why couldn't you stay away and leave us alone?" Michael asked. "Go away daddy. Go away." Michael said with tears running down his face blocking his vision.

"Boy put down that fucking gun or else." Black Ice said. Michael began to shake as he tried to hold the gun steady in his little hands. "Boy did you hear what I told you?" Michael held his breath and used all his might and squeezed the trigger repeatedly. Bang! Bang! Bang! The first two shots hit Black Ice in the chest and the last one in his neck. Black Ice grabbed his neck to stop the blood from gushing out. Black Ice raised his gun and aimed it at Michael. Bang! Bang! Two shots fired simultaneously by both the gun Michael held and Black Ice held. The bullet from Michael's gun went into Black Ice's head killing him instantly, but not before the bullet coming from Black Ice's gun hit Michael's chest sending him flying back.

"No! Lord No!" Rachel screamed as she watched her son get knocked down by the bullet. She used the last of her strength and lifted herself off the floor and limped over Black Ice's body and to Michael, who was squirming on the floor. Rachel knelt down and held Michael in her arms. "It'll be okay baby. Just hold on baby." Rachel cried as she held him closer to her body and began to rack back and forth.

"See mommy I told you I'd protect

you." Michael said and took his last breath and died.

"No! No!" Rachel cried as his body went limp as she continued to hold him and rock back and forth crying.

Chapter 38

"Boy, do you hear me talking to you?" Black Ice said.

Michael snapped back into reality from the vision he was seeing and realized he couldn't leave his mother alone in the world.

"Boy I'm not going to tell you again." Black Ice said.

Michael lowered the gun he was holding.

"That's right boy. Now, I'm going to whip your ass and finish beating your stupid ass mother and her bitch ass cousin." Black Ice walked towards Michael to take the gun out of his hand. All the pain and the hurt he ever felt rushed Michael's body. He raised the gun and repeatedly pulled the trigger.

Black Ice had no time to react as each bullet hit him making him fall over. Michael walked over to his father and watched the blood pour out of him. Rachel watched in shock as her son stood over Black Ice and fired a shot in point blank range into Black Ice's chest killing him. Michael dropped the gun and ran over to his mother.

"I'm coming mommy. I have to get

you and Janet some help." Michael said.

Rachel was barely able to move as her ribs were broken and so was her arm. Janet wasn't in much better shape with one leg broken, a few broken ribs, and blood was still pouring out of her gunshot wound to her shoulder. Rachel knew if she didn't get Janet to the hospital soon she would die from the loss of blood. Rachel used what strength she had to pull Janet up and let her lean on her as they made their way to the front door. Michael held the front door open. He watched as his mother and Janet collapsed at the glass front door.

Police sirens could be heard as the police, ambulance and fire trucks were flying down the street. Michael yelled, "Help! Help! My mommy and Janet need help!"

"Help her first." Rachel said to the rescue squad as she was pointing at Janet who was unconscious.

"What happened here, Miss?" There was a call that shots were fired." The police officer asked.

"He's inside. He tried to hill us, but my son shot him. He's dead." Rachel said.

The officer looked as Michael and wondered how he was able to shoot a grown man. He told the officers what Rachel told him and they rushed into the house while Rachel watched Janet being taken away in the ambulance. Then another ambulance pulled up and the rescue squad came and took Rachel. Michael stay by his mother's side and held his hand.

Before the ambulance pulled off, an officer ran up to the ambulance and asked Rachel, "Miss, what was the man's name that did this?"

"Michael Ice Sr." Rachel replied.

"We found a wallet on a body. It was the only one in there and the ID in the billfold read Jay Jay Conwest. We also found what appeared to be a bulletproof vest with the name Officer Reed stitched in the back of it.

"No! No!" Rachel cried and knew Black Ice got away. "We're never going to be free."

"Don't cry mommy. Don't cry." He said while hugging her and feeling her pain. "We'll be ready for him mommy. We'll be ready." Michael said.

Chapter 39

"We have to control the bleeding. She has lost too much blood." One of the doctors ordered. "We need to do a STAT cesarean section. This lady is pregnant."

When the emergency staff got the woman prepped the doctor gently cut her belly and pulled out the baby. The baby cried as it took its first breath of air. Roxy looked at her baby and whispered the name Michael.

Beep! Beep! Beep! The lifeline monitors on Roxy went flat alarming the emergency crew.

"We're losing her!" The nurse in charge cried out.

"There's nothing we can do for her. She had lost too much blood." The doctor cried as Roxy fell into darkness and death.

Detective Roy watched the whole thing and met the doctor as he walked out of the emergency room.

"You won't be getting any answers from her Detective Roy." The doctor said to him. "She lost too much blood and it's a shame to see a young life lost."

"What about the baby?" Detective Roy inquired.

"The baby is in withdrawal. The poor thing had crack in his system, but in time he will be okay.

"Does she have any family?" Detective Roy asked.

"Not that we know of. I think she named the baby, Michael, before she died. The poor baby will end up in foster care just like any other child of a crack head."

Child of a Crack Head
Part Two

Ten years later, the hustlers on the corner watched her voluptuous body walk down the sidewalk with another man. "Damn shorty, your fine as hell." One of the hustlers yelled out not caring who she was with. The man wrapped his arm around her waist and pulled her closer to him. And they continued to walk down the sidewalk and around the block. As soon as they turned the corner and they were out of sight. He let go of her waist and said, "Bitch didn't I tell you to walk beside me, not in front of me or behind me?" He said as he slapped her so hard in the face that she went flying to the ground.

"But baby, I was walking beside you. I can't help that I have a nice body. The guys are going to look." She said while crying and rubbing her face.

"What? Bitch, you want to talk bad." He bent down and began to punch her furiously in the face and busting her lip and her eye swell shut.

While screaming and crying in pain with each blow, something made the young thug stop his attack on his woman. He turned around to face a man about his age with a machete in his hand.

"Chill Evil this isn't what it looks like. She tripped and fell." He said while pointing to his girl on the concrete crying all curled up in a ball.

"You know the rules." Evil said in a voice that sent chills through the young thug's spine.

"Wait no! No!" He begged and pleaded with his arms out in front of him to keep Evil at a distance. Not knowing that his pleas were upon a cold hearted and a deaf ear.

Evil raised the machete high in the air and came down on the thug's arm and chopped his arm right off. "Ahhh!" The thug screamed as blood gushed out of his detached arm. Evil came down again on the thug's leg chopping it off at the knee. "Ahhh!" He screamed from the pain and saw it only being held together by just a piece of skin. The young thug turned on to his stomach and started crawling away using his good arm as his girl watched in horror as her man made his way to her legs where she was laying on the ground.

"Help me! Help me!" He said in a weak voice.

Evil walked up to him and took off the young thug's fitted hat and bent down and said, "You know my rule." Evil stood back up and swung the machete with all his might and came down on the young thug's neck. Evil kept swinging the machete at his neck until his head rolled off. He picked up the head up and placed it in a bag.

He turned and looked at the frightened woman covered in her man's blood. One of her eyes was swollen shut so she looked at Evil with her good eye. Evil put his bloody hand to his lips and motioned her to be quiet. She knew better than to talk about what happened. She knew Evil would never hit a woman, but we would kill one if he had to.

Michael Ice, Jr., or better known as Evil, walked down the street with a smile on his face with his bag in one hand and a machete in the other. People around the neighborhood knew the rules he had. No hitting on woman in his neighborhood. It didn't matter what age or what they did. He would not see abuse of anymore woman in his lifetime again.

In the shadows, a man with a scar on his face watched the whole thing while smoking on a cigarette stuffed with crack.

He smiled as he watched what the young man did to that thug. It wasn't because he was protecting that woman, but because of the mayhem and the life he took on so easily. He inhaled the cigarette and laughed to himself. "Like father, like son." He said and disappeared into the shadows.

Order Form

Shameek A. Speight

PO BOX 13052

Springfield Gardens, N.Y. 11413

Shameekspeight199@gmail.com

Name	
Address	
City, State, Zip	
Email (via email orders)	
Quantity	
Book Available:	
A Child of a Crack Head	
S&H (via U.S. Priority Mail)	**Price: $3.50**
Total Amount Due	$

Accepted forms of payment are Institutional Checks and Money orders. All mail in orders will take 5-7 business days for delivery. Discounts apply to those incarcerated book price is only $10 plus S&H costs.

Made in the USA
Las Vegas, NV
19 March 2024

87422502R00135